C000091322

CAPTAIN'S SURRENDER
ALEX BEECROFT

Linden Bay Romance, LLC
Palm Harbor, Florida 34684
www.lindenbayromance.com

First Linden Bay Romance publication: January 2008

To Andrew, who believed in me all along. To my family, who are the best. To Lee Rowan, Paola Forti and Säbrinä Mãrie Wadhams, without whom this wouldn't have happened at all. And to all my friends on the web who cheered me on in the writing process and celebrated with me when it was done. Thank you!

Chapter One

Portsmouth Naval Dockyard, 1779.

The bell rang out twice, unbearably sweet. The drums rolled and were silent. As a wind from the sea ruffled the hair of the assembled company, Joshua Andrews looked to one side of the gallows, his eyes unfocused. There was a thunder and rattle as the trapdoor fell open and then, just on the edge of hearing, the snap of a neck and the collective intake of almost five hundred held breaths, as the Nimrods instinctively inhaled to make sure they still could.

"I should say, 'May God have mercy on his soul.'" Captain Walker did not choose to wait even a moment in respect, but clapped his hat back on directly and bestowed a satisfied look upon his crew. "But I know it would be futile. No mercy awaits a man like that, either in this life or the next."

Josh tried not to react, but when Walker's intense gray gaze swept the row of midshipmen, it seemed to pause on him, threatening as a pistol thrust in his face. He made no movement, gave no sign of the panic trying to crawl up his throat, the certainty that Walker *knew,* and fought down the wholly irrational urge to break and run that would be every bit as bad as a confession.

At length, the gaze passed on to terrify the boys standing gape-mouthed and shaken at Josh's right.

"Particularly not on my ship." Hat on, the captain moved down the uncovered ranks of his ship's company, on the alert for movement, for signs of repugnance or weakness, seeming to swim through their fear like a shark. Beside Josh, twelve-year-old Hawkes swayed, face stricken and white, and while Walker's back was turned, Josh reached out and squeezed the child's wrist, setting him upright with a little comforting shake that reassured them both.

Josh, twenty years old and acting lieutenant this past year, was the only oldster among the midshipmen. He found himself at times playing the part of elder brother, even father towards them. It was not a position he particularly relished. Taller than his peers by a good foot and a half, his unlucky red hair uncovered and obvious beneath the sun, and clad—ridiculously—like the other boys, he felt conspicuous enough already without the knowledge of another difference, carried like an invisible brand in the soul.

"Take a good look, lads." Walker's red face was jovial, his eyes in slits of flesh, gleaming with satisfaction. "Whatever your previous captains hushed up for the good of the service, you will not find the same tolerance here. No secrets on my ship. This man was coxswain's mate. Now he's crow bait. Heed the warning."

He began to walk back, past the company of marines, their scarlet uniforms almost obscenely cheerful in this place of execution, past the ship's people, past the lieutenants, and back to the midshipmen. Taking his cane from beneath his elbow, he pushed at their faces with it, angling them until, without closing their eyes, it was impossible for them not to watch Henderson's body jerk and tremble at the end of the rope.

Josh did not wait to be manhandled, but fixed his gaze on his shipmate's shirt-ties and hoped, prayed, that the flailing of limbs and the agonized expression on his face were the result of involuntary spasm, not the signs of a soul in torment. Fear and shame rose up in him. Shame for Henderson, from whose stockinged feet urine dripped—such a neat man in life, and now so stripped of dignity—and for himself. For this was the fate that awaited him should he ever be caught. This was an outward demonstration of the consequences of his vice, the minimum necessary to appease God, before whom he was an abomination.

At the thought his fear turned into anger. He could have done as Portsmouth's urchins were doing on the waterfront—picking up clods of refuse from the shore and pelting Henderson's hanging body with them, shrieking curses. Stupid! It was stupid of the man to have done anything on board, let alone be lured and entrapped by one of Walker's informants. Surely he had known that Walker was the greatest tyrant ever to stand on a quarterdeck, spending ink and energy and vitriol to "clean up" the service. Surely Henderson had known this, and yet he had still been foolish enough to welcome the advances of a shipmate. What could have possessed him? The famine of shipboard life? A death wish? Poor bastard! Poor, stupid, pathetic bastard.

The wind freshened, and the clouds drew away from the sun. A chilly, autumnal light drenched the pale stones of the dockyard and glittered on the sea. Walker's fellow captains of the court martial put on their hats and walked away, talking soberly, the taller bent in an uncomfortable "C" towards the shorter.

Walker tucked his cane beneath his arm once more, light sharp on his gold braid and blazing from the diamond buckles of his shoes. He opened his mouth to speak, and the sound of a carriage interrupted him, coming hell for leather down the quayside, its flamboyant driver plying his whip like a young rake.

Iron shod wheels slid to a stop in fountains of sparks. The Nimrods pretended not to notice as the footman got down and turned the gilded handle of the door. Josh allowed himself to smile as, from the corner of his eye, he saw Walker's complaisance shatter, his brow darken at this affront to his personal piece of theater. All around Josh there was a cautious craning of necks and shifting of positions to see the newcomer, and he had to hiss out of the corner of his mouth to Midshipman Anderson to stop the boy incurring the captain's wrath by actually stepping forward.

Josh found that if he shifted his weight just so, he could watch the unfolding of steps, the brightly polished black shoe and gentleman's leg in a silk stocking descending. There were white breeches and now the skirts of the coat, a deep indigo no less gorgeous for being worn by every officer. There were mariner's cuffs, shiny brass buttons displaying the fouled anchor outlined in heavy gold braid. When fully emerged, the prodigy was revealed as nothing more than another lieutenant of His Majesty's Navy, a parcel of orders clutched to his breast.

Josh should have been disappointed. This was surely the man sent to fill the *Nimrod's* vacant berth, reducing Josh from "acting lieutenant" back down to middie with the rest of them. He should be wrestling with resentment, hating the sight of the man. But for some reason he could not quite manage it.

Saluting, the stranger introduced himself. He was very tall and slender, his face all angles and bones, with clear, sea green eyes into which the illumination of the autumn sun seemed to pour. Or perhaps it was the clarity of his spirit that shone out as he smiled depreciatingly at Walker's purple wrath.

"Captain Walker? My apologies! The axle cracked outside Kidderminster, and on the road through Weston we were waylaid by highwaymen. My watch said five to the hour as we entered the yard, so I had them crack on as fast as they could. I hope I am not late?"

Automatically, Walker checked his timepiece. His

mouth thinned into a stroke of wire as he held out a mute hand for the orders. Not allowing himself to wilt beneath the glare, the young man handed them over, straightened his shoulders and stood impassively while Captain Walker checked them.

"Not *late,* Mr. Kenyon," said Walker, at length, with a cold fury that made the young man's smile fall away and his expression harden. "But you are a damned abominable coxcomb, arriving in this manner. You have missed your profession, sir—the navy does not exist as a backdrop for your theatricals. What do you mean by it?"

Around Josh a sense of thankfulness rose off the crew. The heavy gaze of officialdom had been shifted from their backs. Henderson still trembled, swaying pendulum-like on his gibbet, but the trembling of the living eased and there broke out, here and there, the reluctant smiles of those who are glad this was happening to someone else.

Josh was overwhelmed by a sensation he had never felt before. Lt. Kenyon had bowed his head to study the cobbles by Walker's feet, and Josh found himself fascinated by the elegant curve of his neck and by the refined white hands lying in the small of his back. He was captivated, too, by Kenyon's shoulders—narrow but lithe—and his black brows and lashes, so startling under the white wig.

Josh badly wanted to do something to encourage the man to move again, so lightly he had descended from the carriage. How would he walk? How would he hold himself if he were to dance? He looked as though he should dance. Hell, with the fine poise of him, he looked as though he should fly; unfurl a great pair of white-feathered wings like the Archangel Michael and fly.

"I meant nothing, sir, but desired to be here at my appointed time. As you see, the hospital would not release Lt. Ollerton. There have been complications. And as I must be in Bermuda as soon as is humanly possible, it seemed good to all that I should take his place." The green eyes swept up, not at all abashed, but honestly concerned. "Were you not informed?"

"God's blood, man! Do you question me? Will I have to bring you to a proper subordination, Mr. Kenyon? I should have thought the object lesson behind me would induce you to remember your place."

Though he had not known there was such a person all of five minutes ago, something twisted in Josh's throat at the thought of Kenyon on the gallows. What was bitter with Henderson, beside whom he had worked for three years, would be sheer blasphemy in the case of this stranger. But why? Why would he almost rather feel the rope about his own neck? How was that possible? What... What was the matter with him? He didn't even know the man!

Confused and a little frightened by the strength of this...whatever it was, Josh looked away, then back, and by chance he caught Kenyon's gaze as it swept the rows of silent men, looking for support or advice. Kenyon was older than him, certainly, his face settled into adult lines, but his eyes...oh. Oh, they were like a pool of fresh water in the desert. Josh had not known before how thirsty he was, how he yearned for that cool, for that refreshment. His mouth fell open; he took a half step forward. Kenyon smiled an uncertain, polite smile, which filled his chest with sunlight, and his lips had twitched in answer, involuntary, when Walker laughed.

It was a cynical, sudden bark of laughter, as humorous as the report of a pistol, and it shocked through Josh in much the same way. The fragile moment of joy disappeared under terror. *He knows nothing! He has no proof! I was just smiling! Mother of God, what came over me? What was I thinking?*

He looked back at the corpse, as if for council. Its protruding eyes seemed to mock him, as if to say, "Do you still think me so stupid now?" He breathed in shakily, appalled. Was this what Henderson had felt for the

6

informer? This tie of the soul, this abandonment of all caution, as though nothing else existed in the world but the two of them?

Josh had been at sea since he was thirteen, had not mixed in the most refined company, and did not believe in love at first sight. More than that, he had never heard that sodomites were capable of love. Since childhood, he had heard that he was a beast, driven by perverted appetites, not a rational being whose heart could be moved by beauty or lifted by a smile. He was not *worthy* to love this fine young officer, not even to admire him from afar.

But—Mary and Joseph—suppose it *was* love! How fitting to fall in love in the shadow of the gallows. Watching Henderson finally settle into stillness on the end of his rope, he tried to resist the urge to look back at Lt. Kenyon as he might have tried to resist the urge to breathe. When he gave up, allowed himself a stealthy glance, he found that Walker was watching him with the gleam of triumph in his eye.

The steady world fell out from beneath his feet. For such a long time he had been sure of his self-restraint, certain that whatever the captain suspected, he could prove nothing. Now Walker was watching him with the pleasure of a fisherman who has finally discovered the right bait.

"Well, Mr. Kenyon," Walker said in a more amiable tone, "you are very welcome. Since Comptroller Summersgill and his household are to travel with us, I have ceded him the Great Cabin and taken the first lieutenant's cabin myself, but I'm sure we will find somewhere to lodge you where you will be appreciated as you deserve. Do not hesitate to call on me if you find anything...irregular. I like to run a clean ship."

Noting the limpness of Henderson's corpse, Walker swept the assembled company with a glare, calling them to attention. "We sail with the tide. On board, the lot of you. Dismissed."

Josh turned to run back to the ship with the other boys,

hoping to get away, just for a few moments, just for enough time to collect himself. But he was certain in the pit of his stomach that he would not be allowed.

"Andrews!"

Stopping, he concentrated on looking innocently surprised. "Take Mr. Kenyon's dunnage to your cabin, Andrews. I'm sure you will have no objections to him as a bedfellow, eh?"

Don't blush. Do not dare! But he could feel it, flooding up his fair skin from neck to brow like the mark of Cain. Please, God, let Kenyon only think it was a reaction to the innuendo. He did not dare to look. "Aye, aye, sir," he said instead, and with the help of Kenyon's footman, he got the sea-chest off the ground and up the gangplank to the ship.

Josh's cabin was larger than the fourth lieutenant's coffin of a room by virtue of having one of the great guns inside it. The cannon was a familiar presence, tied up tight to the wall and used as a clothes horse. When he had put down Kenyon's sea-chest as snugly beside it as was possible, and had removed his spare shirts and his shaving gear from its top, the cabin no longer looked so homely. The blue painted chest—silhouettes of three frigates carefully drawn in roundels on its sides—was disconcertingly real. Touching it again, he revealed that it was as solid as ever, and that its owner, therefore, must also have some reality beyond Josh's nervous imagination.

Sending one of the boys to request a second hanging cot, he sat down on his bed and stared at the box, his mind in turmoil. How could this be happening? They would be a month at sea, if not longer, and he would be shut in here every night with a man who had already made him betray himself worse than he had managed to do in the whole of his seven year service. Josh had no illusions—having tasted one success, Walker wanted Josh's neck in the noose next and was counting on Kenyon as the way to achieve it.

And there sat Kenyon's sea-chest, as colorful, as neat

and as large as life as the man himself. The man who might even now be heading here from the quarterdeck or the wardroom, to whom Josh would have to make polite conversation, while his mind raced and his pulse thundered from the glory. Josh could imagine—oh, how he could imagine!—what it would be like to lie close in here with that tall, elegant form sprawled in the cot above him. Maybe an arm dangling down into his space, the scent of cologne and new linen, and himself lying beneath with a guilty conscience and an aching prick, wanting to feel the long fingers on his skin, suck each one into his mouth and...

Oh, now look! Damn it—that was all he needed. Could he not control his wandering thoughts at all? *Think of something else!* Perhaps living together would wear the edge off this infatuation. All he knew of Kenyon, after all, was that he moved like an angel. Suppose he snored, and his feet smelled, and his politics were abominable, and he never shut up? Suppose he was all flash and show, as Walker seemed to think? Being closely confined with him then might be a cure.

Would be a cure, Josh ignored the part of himself that clamored for some sort of fairytale ending. There was no hope that his affections could be returned. Even if he liked Kenyon, he would not be able to trust him. Not with such a secret as this. As Henderson could attest, such things did not happen to men like himself, particularly not when Captain Walker was stalking them. No. Josh was no man's victim. He could not afford to hope for love. He wanted to live, and he *would*.

The wooden edges of his cot dug into his thighs, making his feet go numb. Through the gun-port he could see Mr. Summersgill's party making their final farewells, his wife clutching her many shawls and weeping with fright at the prospect of the voyage.

His ward, a fair haired, vivacious girl—orphaned daughter of some cousin, if wardroom rumor was to be believed—gazed up at the ship with inquisitive intelligence, and Josh leaned forward to see better as Kenyon came up beside her. It was a thrill merely to watch him as he passed unawares along the quay beneath. He spoke. She laughed in return, and they walked up the gangplank, out of Josh's sight, looking beautiful together. Josh clamped his teeth closed so tightly that pain lanced through his face and into his eyes as he tried to tell himself that this, too, was what he wanted.

It was better that love should die, rather than that *he* should. Better that Kenyon should be inaccessible, paying court to someone else. It was better for them all that this should end before it could even have been said to begin. Of course it was.

The decision made, lying heavily within him, he rubbed his eyes and was about to put his hat back on and return to work when there came a knock on the door, and the man himself leaned in, his eyebrows raised and his extraordinary eyes almost hazel in the between decks' gloom. "Hello? May I come in?"

Josh scrambled to his feet, forgetting everything, even his name, cracked his head against the reinforced beam above him, everything going interestingly gray and silver for a moment. "Um..." he said, "I... Oh, I..." And Kenyon came in.

Chapter Two

Dearest Mother, Peter Kenyon wrote carefully—for the *Nimrod* was skipping through a stiff sea that made her massive bulk frisk like a spring lamb. *You will be glad to know that we are three weeks out from Portsmouth and, although delayed by storms, are in hopes of catching the trade winds within a day or so. Should nothing very untoward happen, I hope to be in Bermuda by this time next month.*

He paused, looked out of the gun-port at the gray seas and the white spray blowing forward through the long, slanting rain, and honesty prompted him to add; *Though, God knows, there is no certainty in this profession.*

Mr. Summersgill and his wife, he went on, *were just overcoming the sea-sickness when we hit the present seven-day blow, which prostrated them again. Doubtless, they would ask to be remembered to you if they could speak without groaning.*

His practiced ear caught the slow scaling down of the wind's note in the rigging, and the weather that came through the newly opened port contained more air than water now. The floor of the cabin was almost dry, and the once soaked blankets of his bed were merely damp to the touch. *But the storm eased last night and continues to abate, so I am in hopes that they will recover soon.*

Dipping his quill, he wondered if he should be

circumspect, but this was his mother. What she did not know, she would guess. Little point then in being coy.

I did not know that Mr. Summersgill had a ward, which seems a remarkable lack of perception on my part since I grew up within an hour's walk of his house. Do I dare too much if I guess she is the "natural child" whose birth is still being talked of in hushed voices eighteen years later?

The smile grew wider as he thought of her. She had not been laid low by illness and, without supervision, had run a little wild, even to the extent of putting on Lt. Sanderson's white duck trousers and climbing to the masthead. She had been so aglow with the experience that—with the enthusiasm bringing a pretty flush to her face, her golden hair streaming, and the thrillingly transgressive sight of her legs and her ass so flagrantly revealed by the close-fitting garments—he would be surprised if there was a single man on board who was not now her abject slave.

His own admiration, however, he felt was more rational. He was a third son, of no great account, and while his eldest brother Charles might be constrained to marry an heiress for the good of the estates, he himself could afford to choose who he wished. It was true that his fortune was yet to be made and he had no thought of supporting a wife on a lieutenant's meager salary. But once he had made post captain, and was secure enough, why not wed the daughter of an old family friend? Whatever her mother's status, if it secured him the continued influence and good wishes of the Comptroller of HM Customs and Excise in Bermuda, so much the better.

After a long pause to relive the mast climbing incident and decide that it was something he did not wish to share with his mother, he went on. *She is, at any rate, a most attractive and spirited girl and will have better prospects in Bermuda than if she remains where her shame is known.*

A scuffle of feet above his head broke his concentration. He looked up but, of course, could see nothing more than the thick planks of the deck and the unlit lantern. A voice he had already learned to loathe called out. "You! You call this rope coiled? Boatswain, start this man! No, damn it—with some feeling in it!"

Even through two inches of mahogany planking, Peter could hear the snap and thud of a rope's end hitting flesh. Then the mumble of "Beg pardon sir, but I was splicing the rope afore a coiling of it, on account of it got tore up something terrible during the blow."

He found himself holding his breath, waiting for the answer, and when it came, he closed his eyes for fear of revealing, even to the darkness and the sleeping man who shared his cabin, the building contempt within him.

"By God, I will have no answering back from you! Take this man's name. A dozen strokes to remind him who is the captain of this vessel, and I want to see every rope on this deck fit for an admiral's inspection, or I will add another forty for slovenliness."

There was a rustle, and he opened his eyes to find that Andrews had woken, raised himself on one elbow and was watching him. His softly curling red hair was flattened to his skull on one side and sleep grimed the corners of his brown eyes, but his expression was alert enough. Peter recognized the look on Andrews' face as the mirror of his own disgust. Silently, they shared a moment of perfect understanding. Then Peter looked down, and Andrews— who had rested barely five hours in the last seven days, on constant duty in the rigging—turned over to face the wall, pulled the blanket up over his ears, and fell back to sleep at once.

I wish I could be equally enthusiastic about the ship, Peter paused, wondering if even his private correspondence was safe. It was a mark of how quickly he had learned to adapt to the atmosphere of paranoia on the *Nimrod* that he thought Walker might go through his letters. Though it was an unheard of thing to suspect, it was also unheard of that a first lieutenant should be expected to share his cabin with a midshipman, no matter how senior. That had been an insult—a deliberate, calculated insult—and the fact that he could not challenge his captain did not mean he had forgotten or forgiven it.

To be fair to Andrews, one of the first things he had done—when he finally got over his tongue-tied shyness—had been to offer to move out. It was to the young man's credit that, though he had grown accustomed to the privacy, and faced a removal back into the fetid cockpit of boys' practical jokes and nastiness that was the midshipmen's berth, he had still offered it with such sincerity. No, Peter did not resent Andrews in the slightest for the arrangement. He knew perfectly well who to blame.

If you recall, we were told that Captain Walker ran "a taut ship". Loyalty prevents me from saying much more than this; if matters aboard were any tauter, they would snap. I am thankful that for me this is but a temporary post, and my own command awaits me in St. George, but I am concerned for the fate of my current shipmates, who do not have that consolation.

The thought of another wardroom dinner was oppressive. He had tried his hardest to encourage conversation at the table, broaching every irreproachable topic from the weather to the perfidy of the French, and it had all met with murmurs of anxious agreement and then silence.

The second lieutenant, Lt. Cole, could be drawn out to admit to attending plays in London but would falter and look suspiciously down the length of the table when asked what they were about. Lt. Sanderson, his opposite in looks—a savagely dark, scrawny looking man, who seemed to regard ship's biscuit as something of an extravagance— shared the reluctance to commit himself to an opinion on anything. The other members of the ward room, Stapleton, the sergeant of marines, Lt. Bendick, Lt. Harcourt, and Dr.

O'Connor, no matter how pressed, had simply not spoken at all.

By the end of the first week, Peter was finding it difficult to get through his meals without losing his temper and flying out upon their dullness and their timidity. He had been made so peevish and so reckless by it, so disheartened by the lack of community, and—frankly—so *lonely*, that in his own cabin he had forgotten himself and made a cutting remark about being surrounded by ghosts and old women.

Which had been when Mr. Andrews—after a week of stuttering and running away—had suddenly begun to speak to him. "You do know, sir," he had said quietly, "that the captain has his informers in every level of the ship, and no one's sure who they are? He hears everything, and he pays back what he doesn't like threefold. There isn't one of us on board who isn't afraid."

"If a man does his job to the best of his ability, he should have no cause to be afraid!" Peter had replied indignantly, and Andrews laughed, a cynical little smirk replacing the blush and look of panic that had heretofore been his permanent expression.

"You'd think so, wouldn't you? Not on the *Nimrod* though, sir. We eat our own."

This dark and rather Celtic observation—hovering ominously on the edge of meaning—came back to him now, less for its warning than for the surge of relief and delight he had felt at having finally discovered an ally on this unhappy ship. It was the first gesture of friendship that he had received on board, and he treasured it. He treasured it, indeed, so much that when Andrews had followed it up by offering to remove himself from the cabin, he had not had to think twice about saying no.

Resting the feather of his quill against his cheek, he looked up meditatively at the sleeping man, just as the rain eased and a slice of sunshine lanced unexpectedly through the porthole, making Andrews' hair blaze like copper and fire. Idly, Peter wondered why it was thought to be such an unattractive color, for he found it very pleasing. There was an unearthliness about it, perhaps, which made him feel as though Andrews existed partly in a different world from himself. A feeling that only increased when he discovered the midshipman had a large repertoire of Irish folk tales and could be persuaded to share them, late at night, when he was halfway through his second bottle of wine and thoroughly hidden in the darkness.

Peter dipped his quill and brought it to hover over the page, meaning to write; *nevertheless, I have been fortunate enough to make the acquaintance of a valuable young man, whom I hope soon to count as a friend. He is already an ally.* But something persuaded him to hold off—a wish not to tempt fate, perhaps, or the conviction that his mother would not be interested in such small details.

Instead he laid the pen down in its place in his writing box, took out the silver and glass shaker, and shook sand over his letter, drying the ink. Folding it rather than putting it in the box where it belonged, he set it inside a book and tucked the book into the center of a pile of neatly folded stockings in his sea chest, feeling ridiculously cloak and dagger but unwilling to take the risk that anyone could find it. A man like Walker, who could flog a seaman for being diligent enough to repair damaged rope before coiling it, would not hesitate to use even the mild dissatisfaction of his letter as evidence of mutinous thoughts.

He closed the sea chest softly, as if that too might be a crime. *Mutinous thoughts?* As he set his wig carefully on top of his own black hair and his hat upon that, he almost felt he was drawing a cover over revolution, holding it down. For God's sake! He had been aboard less than three weeks—he could not judge in that time. Nor was it his business to criticize how a captain ran his own ship. A man's ship was his kingdom, and if Walker's was an unhappy one, what of it? It was no excuse for rebellion.

How would the service operate without order, without obedience, without...*tyranny*?

Carefully, so as not to disturb Andrews' well earned rest a second time, he padded out into the wardroom, leaning back for a moment on the closed door as if he could trap the treasonous thoughts inside. Clearly he had been reading too much in the papers about the war in the Americas, and the colonists' notions of self rule and justice for all. He had been infected by revolutionary fervor, but it would not do. It would not do. Not in the Navy. So he preferred a happy ship? What of it? If an unhappy ship worked as well, it was no business of his to contemplate overturning the established order. He was appalled at himself for even thinking it.

Truly appalled—for when he straightened up he found that his hands were trembling and his heart racing within him. His conscience felt tender and swollen, as though his guilt was obvious to all. Fortunately, however, those who were not needed on deck were asleep, recovering from the storm, and he had time to breathe deeply, smooth the creases of his cravat, and gather himself, unobserved.

But, as first lieutenant, it *was* his business, he decided, to do what he could to minimize that unhappiness. He could set the ship in such good order that Walker would have no reason to tyrannize. He could protect the ship's people by making them as perfect as it was humanly possible to be, and that he would do with all the strength in him.

The wardroom presented a post-storm squalor of half eaten cold dishes of food, abandoned oilcloths, drowsing servants, and drying pools of water. Lt. Harcourt was there, asleep in a chair with his head pillowed on his folded arms and a self-satisfied rat gnawing on a chicken bone by his hand. This, for a start, needed to be rectified. Peter woke the servants and set them to clean, woke Harcourt and sent him off to his cabin to sleep in private, and then went on deck to supervise the coiling of ropes and satisfy himself that no rational mind would see fit to order those extra forty strokes.

Peter Kenyon was not an inconsiderable officer, indeed he believed himself to be extremely capable. He had a series of successes behind him of which he was justly proud, and he would do what he could. He only hoped it would be enough.

Chapter Three

Sunlight fell on the pages of Emily Jones' book, surprising her. Putting it down on the side of her cot, she looked up. For the first time in days, the arch of the stern windows showed clear rain-washed skies, purple and charcoal storm-clouds retreating towards a now almost mythical England, so far away.

Flinging her feet out of bed, the oilcloth covered floor springy and warm beneath her bare feet, she caught sight of her father's wife, buried under shaking blankets, and the feeble movements in the hammock where her father lay suffering, and—for their sake—refrained from dancing at the excitement of it all.

The wooden world in which they were all confined rose and fell with each wave, which she had expected. What she had not expected was the side to side roll and the irregular speeding and slowing depending on the wind. These three oscillations combined to result in the ship proceeding with a motion like a hesitant corkscrew—up, down, left, right, and forward, all at the same time. Emily found this thrilling, like the motions of a country dance, but she could plainly see it was not so pleasant for everyone.

There was no sign of her maid, Bess, but after the girl's heroic service, mopping, running about with malodorous buckets, administering wine and water, laudanum, and cool cloths, Emily did not grudge her a morning off. It was easy enough to dress in an old gown and twist her hair into a plain bun beneath a firmly pinned hat.

With a glance of sympathy for the sufferers, she let herself out of the cabin and onto the quarterdeck. There the breeze attempted to fling her bonnet over the rail. She clutched it and looked up to where sunlight burst brilliantly on the concavities of white sail. The air smelled fresh after the cabin's reek of sickness, and the deck beneath her feet was clean enough for a ballroom—lines of dazzling white wood and gleaming black pitch.

On either side of the great wheel, two men with checked shirts and long, swinging pigtails stood, gentling the huge ship on her course. Neither so much as glanced over his shoulder at the sound of the cabin door closing. But several officers turned to look at her forbiddingly. There was no echo to her hopeful smile in a single face, and despite the calm immensity of light she felt an oppression such as she had experienced all too often among those who blamed her for her father's immorality. The vinegar faces told her the captain was on deck, for they were none of them so unfriendly when he was below.

Turning, she saw him at the far side of the quarterdeck, standing in splendid isolation, glaring up at something about the sails which affronted him. A heavy man, with a ruddy face deeply grooved with disapproval, he was the epitome of cleanliness from his snowy wig to his highly polished shoes.

Though there were above fifty men visible, scrubbing, polishing, coiling rope, there was no sound of voices. The great ship forged her way onwards in silence through the bright day as though there were no live thing on board.

Emily supposed that she should greet the captain, make the effort to thank him for getting them through the terrifying weather. Just because he was an ass didn't mean that she should be, after all. So she braced herself and walked forward, prepared to be amiable. But as she passed the wheel, Walker turned and gave her a vicious glare—as nakedly aggressive and as shocking as a slap in the face.

Reeling away, exactly as though she had been slapped, she collided with her father, who had emerged from the cabin just in time to see the exchange. His face was white with fury and then green. Turning, he ran for the rail but could not quite make the distance before being comprehensively sick over the gleaming, proudly scrubbed decks.

She rushed to his side, hearing an oath behind her and the sound of hurrying feet. By the time he had taken her proffered handkerchief and could look up, holding it to his mouth, a noseless, toothless tar—one of the common sailors—had come running, a large bucket of seawater carried effortlessly in his sinewy hands. As she helped her father to scramble back to his feet, the sailor gave them both his own scouring look of utter contempt.

"Fuckin' jobbernowl lubber! Which it took me fuckin' hours this mornin' a-scrubbin 'til me fuckin' knees *bled* t' get this clean. Will 'e fuckin clean it up himself? No 'e will not. Fuckin' grass-combing arsy-versy silver-spoon-in-'is-mouth Molly Clap's beau."

The feeling of being attacked from all sides was too much. Emily found herself shaking with fury, tears welling and threatening to fall, outraged on her father's behalf, and powerless to do anything about it. Her father himself, unshaven and cadaverous from a fortnight without food and still an interesting shade of green, had opened his mouth to deliver a cutting retort, when one of the officers strode across the quarterdeck in three long paces and cracked the sailor such a blow across the back with a stout cane that it drove him to his knees. A second blow landed on the man's shoulder, and a third on his face, overbalancing him. Tumbling backwards over the pail, he went sprawling—his eye already swelling—into the vomit. Covering his head with his hands, he cringed and whined as the last whistling crack drove into his belly, smacking all the breath out of him.

Coughing and whooping for air, he curled up tightly, trying to make himself small, but the officer insinuated the end of his cane between shoulder and bruised cheek and pressed, turning the man's head, forcing him to look up.

"This is George Summersgill, His Majesty's Comptroller of Bermuda. Soldier, statesman, our guest, and a man old enough to be your father. On every single count deserving of respect. You will apologize. Then you will further apologize to this young lady, whose ears have been offended by your profanity."

Angry though she had been, such casual brutality shocked Emily. She looked at the man who had come to their rescue with a sort of horror, while her father straightened himself and closed his eyes briefly to hide the terrible nausea and his weakness.

"He *is* a..." the sailor muttered.

Throughout the beating there had been no glimmer of human feeling on the young officer's face. Now, for the first time, there was a touch of something more personal, guarded until it was almost indecipherable. Frustration, perhaps. "Bates, are you *asking* me to take your name?"

Whatever it was, the sailor appeared to understand it. He closed his mouth and dragged himself to his feet. Staggering a little, he knuckled the side of his forehead that was not purple with spreading bruises. "Sorry, squire. I'm a crossgrained bugger at times, don'tee pay no mind. Nor you, fine missy. You want a thing, just call for Bates an 'e'll 'op to it right smart, aye?"

"Are you satisfied, sir?"

Emily was about to say, "No, not at all!" when the most astonishing thing happened. Her father opened his eyes and smiled a weak but genuinely warm smile at the newcomer. "Thank you, Peter. You may dismiss the man, I accept his apology. The true injury was elsewhere."

The stick rested on the sailor's blackened cheek for a moment, while the young officer looked down like an owner at his slave. "Get this cleaned up then. And, Bates... Don't trespass on my kindness again. I cannot always be so forgiving."

As Bates swabbed the foul mixture of sea-water and sick from the deck, leaping down to the waist of the ship to refill his bucket, the officer folded his hands behind his back and drew himself up. He was a young man who might have been handsome had there been any affability about his countenance, his eyes brownish green and stony as chips of jade. They softened as he looked at Emily and, tucking the cane under his left arm, he held out an elegant hand and smiled. "But we haven't been introduced. First Lieutenant Peter Kenyon. My family's estate borders that of your guardian. I must apologize again on behalf of my ship. We have none of us slept for the past week—running before the storm. I know that's no excuse but..."

"Please." It was painful to Emily to receive this gallantry even while she could see the terrible marks of the man's violence blooming on Bates' face. She knew, of course, that men were violent, but the easy ferocity, coming on top of that dreadful, murderous glare, made her feel conscious of the scarcely leashed brutality on board. She was one of only three women among eight hundred men. Pleasantries that might have been flattering in an assembly room full of other girls became difficult to negotiate, almost threatening in this atmosphere. "Please, it's quite all right. I'm an ignorant traveler in your world—I must expect to offend at all turns. I dare say I shall learn better in time."

She took the offered hand, surprised to find it quite clean—not bloodstained at all. Surprised, too, that he did not presume to raise it to his lips but only bowed over it civilly.

"You should certainly have been told that the windward side of the quarterdeck is sacrosanct. *No one* treads there

23

but the captain. It's a tradition so old we forget sometimes that not everyone is born knowing it."

"Have I offended terribly?"

"Not at all," Kenyon said with conviction. On closer examination, there seemed to be something about him in conflict with Emily's initial impression, and now his lean face broke into a small smile, self conscious, rather sweet. "You were...prevented, after all."

"Prevented," her father broke in with a self-depreciating laugh, "well, yes, and I am to suppose that being in the fire is preferable to being in the frying pan?"

Kenyon's smile widened. "I could name you several admirals who suffer from the same affliction, sir. It's the neatness of the decks that occupies our minds. Next time, over the side or—in extremis—into your hat, and no one will think the worse of you."

This was a comfort, and receiving comfort at this young man's hands was something of a puzzle. It was hard for Emily to reconcile the Kenyon of the cane with the Kenyon of the smile. She had almost considered asking him how he himself held the two together just as Edwards' voice croaked out behind them like the boom of a bittern.

"Mr. Kenyon, when you are done toadying, might you spare a second's attention to your tasks?"

There had been a thawing, a change of those green eyes from ice to liquid, so slight that Emily noticed it now only when it was withdrawn, and Kenyon again became all edges—inhumanly cold. He bowed stiffly and withdrew, and she found herself relieved to have him gone.

"Emily," her father chided her gently, "Peter is a fine young gentleman, whatever you might think. Had he not intervened, I would have been forced to punish the man myself. Let these people show contempt to you once, and you will never regain their respect."

"I understand, sir," she said and curtsied, feeling grateful to him that he had at least *tried* to come to her

24

defense against the captain and responsible that he had lost so much countenance in failing. But she wondered, nevertheless, quite where a bastard stood in the scheme of things. She was not wholly sure she was not one of "these people" herself.

Thoroughly unsettled, and in the absence of other women to whom she could honestly open her mind, she decided to visit the ship's boys where she would at least have the comfort of being an adult among children. "Father, I've been having lessons with the midshipmen. The science of navigation has become my fascination. Oh, and Hawkes wishes to show me his pet rat—he says it is the size of a kitten—may I go?"

Her father smiled one of his sly, statesmanlike smiles— the one that indicated he already knew all her thoughts and approved, but could not, for reasons of good government, possibly say so aloud. "You will do whatever you please, my dear. As you always do. And I...I think I need breakfast, and after that the nearest thing to a bath that can be arranged."

He returned to the cabin, and Emily went down into the warm, dark fug in the belly of the ship, wondering about Kenyon.

"Toadying" Captain Walker had said, and though she had no great respect for his opinions, this one had some plausibility. There was good reason for a man of ambition to toady to her father. If that was so, he had certainly succeeded in taking her father in, but he would find her a harder nut to crack.

She had been Summersgill's "ward" now for all of three months, but that time had been long enough to introduce her to the novel idea that she had become highly desirable in the marriage market. Men who had not looked at her twice when she was plain "Miss Jones from the milliners" positively fawned on Miss Summersgill-Jones. It had been flattering, at first, but that had worn off sometime after the second ball, when she realized that none of them were seeing *her* at all.

It probably was ridiculous of her to want to marry for love, but it was not ridiculous to want to marry someone who would treat her well and make her happy. This man, with his easy brutality and cold, shuttered eyes would do neither, and with his plausible manners he would deny her even the sympathy of her friends. True, he had not importuned her yet, but there had been an anxiousness in his look, and she felt sure it was only a matter of time.

As she opened the flimsy partition door into the gunroom and made admiring noises over the rat, she touched the damp, working sides of the ship and thought that in this matter she, too, was a man-of-war, readying herself for the onslaught of the enemy.

Summersgill, a distant, but an affectionate and dutiful father, had evidently decided it was now time to make sure his daughter was settled with a man who would offer her the life to which Summersgill felt she was entitled. She was sensible enough to be grateful for that. But when the time came, she fully intended to give herself to the man of her choice, not to be taken as a prize, whatever her father and his neighbors' children might have to say about it.

Chapter Four

"Mr. Hawkes, let us suppose it is heavy weather, the fog is so thick that you cannot see the other ships of the fleet. What is the admiral's signal to bring to and lie by, with head-sails to the mast, with the starboard tack aboard?"

"Um..."

Mr. Hawkes was a boy who greatly resembled his rat, Summersgill thought as he sat in the gunroom reading his predecessor's reports of French privateers about the shores of Bermuda, his fears of an invasion by American forces, and the roaring illegal trade in weapons smuggled to those same forces for huge amounts of money in defiance of all self interest and principle.

Across the table from him Bess, now recovered, darned stockings and kept her head down. Emily was sitting in front of a slate, in common with five of the rapscallions known as "young gentlemen". Boys who looked to Summersgill scarcely old enough to be in breeches.

"Mr. Hawkes, please say something before we begin to grow barnacles."

"He'll fire eight guns, sir."

"You're on the reef, Mr. Hawkes. Your ship has just sunk with all hands, and when they write home to your poor, weeping mother they will say 'if only he'd paid more attention in his classes'. And Mr. Anderson? If you wipe your nose on your cuff one more time, I will cut it off and give it to you as a keepsake."

The senior midshipman—a Mr. Andrews—in charge of this little school was himself a youth barely old enough to be at university, who kept the boys in check by his ready, sarcastic wit, without reliance either on the cane or profanity. On this first examination, Summersgill was satisfied that he could leave Emily here to be occupied without having to fear for her moral safety or her delicacy of mind.

"On the starboard tack he will fire six guns. Eight for larboard. Enough; everything away before muster, now."

The schoolroom was packed away in the blink of an eye, and the boys were neatening themselves, tensely earnest, when drums began hammering on every deck. The boys were out of the door before Summersgill had time to stand up, their teacher grabbing his coat with one hand and straightening his neck-cloth with the other.

"Is it a battle?" said Summersgill, wondering if he had time to run to his cabin for his sword.

"No, sir, just muster." Andrews stopped and looked at him with an anxious expression. "All hands to witness punishment. The ladies should go down to the hold."

"What is so shameful that I am not permitted to see?" asked Emily caustically, rising and putting her slate away in a large bag.

"Not shameful, miss." The midshipman spared her a glance—and now he noticed it, it was surprising how little the lad had looked at her and how lacking in admiration was his gaze now. Summersgill approved; the boy obviously knew his place. "Just an unpleasantness you'd do better to be spared."

He turned a dark, meaningful gaze on Summersgill. "It isn't a fit sight, sir. Frankly, I'd keep the boys down here, too, if I could." Having struggled into his coat as he was speaking, he twitched it straight and shivered slightly. "I must go. Please, you really don't want her to see. Believe me."

"Go down to the hold, Emily," Summersgill said, his heart sinking. "You too, Bess. My wife will be glad of the company—you know how she gets in confined spaces. We must...respect the customs of the sea." Privately, he felt that this was a great fuss about nothing. Emily—who had attended hangings since she was ten—was no shrinking miss to be spared the sight of crime's due punishment.

The silence on deck as he came out into the wind made his confidence falter. Hangings were social occasions, full of the common solidarity of the honest, and the sense of heightened life that came from being so near to death. Here there was none of that. The same despair he had felt onboard from the first now mantled a hundred fold over the gleaming lines of men, casting an irony over their beautifully laundered best Sunday clothes and a shadow over every resentful face.

One of the gratings which covered hatchways had been set upright, and now Henry Addings, convicted of "answering back", was secured to it with rough cables. The boatswain was handed a red bag and withdrew the famous cat of nine tails—a nasty looking object with its long thongs greased so they would cut deeper.

"Ready, sir."

"Five dozen," said Walker with a look of anticipation. "And lay on with a will."

Henry Addings did not scream until the thirtieth stroke. By the fortieth he had lost consciousness and hung like a freshly slaughtered carcass from his restraints, a pool of blood spreading about his feet, white gleams of backbone and ribs showing through the lace-work of his flesh. The boatswain switched arms to prevent himself from growing tired, the officers looking on with blank, indifferent faces. Walker licked his lips. Summersgill raised his handkerchief to his mouth and bit his forefinger. As a distraction, it did not help.

"Jabe Aken. Maliciously and persistently slow in the execution of his duties." An undernourished looking creature who walked away from the beating, whimpering and slower than ever.

"Perseverance Atkins. Last man down from the studdingsail booms on three separate occasions Thursday."

It dawned on Summersgill with horror that they were working their way through the alphabet. The deck was already aswim with blood, pouring into the scuppers and thence to the sea. The boatswain and his mates had taken off their shoes and rolled up their trouser-legs to stop themselves slipping in it. The wind had dropped away and the warm reek of gore rose over the quarterdeck, cut with ammonia as Atkins pissed himself on the forty-first stroke.

"Joe Bainsford. Last man down from the masthead Thursday."

Joe Bainsford had the long plait, the silk scarf, and ribbon-embroidered trousers that had been pointed out to Summersgill as the identifying signs of a long-term career sailor—worth his weight in gold to the king. Hearing his name, an almost inaudible growl went through the massed ranks of men.

"Arthur Berry. Answering back and slovenly treatment of the ship's ropes."

Berry screamed from the first stroke, the noises growing progressively more and more bestial until Summersgill wanted to stop his ears, to close his eyes, to pretend he was back on land. No wonder Peter had shocked him so by displaying a harshness Summersgill had not known the man possessed. Appalled did not even begin to describe what he felt.

The faces on the quarterdeck were hardly less inhuman than those in the waist of the ship, fixed in attitudes of sheer indifference. Only the boys—standing by their divisions—trembled or smiled as their natures dictated, the larval forms of the stern or gloating tyrants they would one day become.

The count moved on too slowly, and Summersgill looked away to the sea for comfort. But even there this ritual was grotesquely mirrored. Sharks kept pace with the ship, their bodies blue in the clear water, dashing and snapping in frenzy at the blood.

"Patrick Hare. Papist blasphemy and expressing opinions sympathetic to the Irish rebellion."

Patrick Hare was gagged with a metal spike that split his lips open on both sides and made him drool blood. His back was already raw—scabbed and half healed from a previous punishment.

"Spreading sedition is a crime against the whole ship's company," said Walker, stirring out of a kind of trance of glory—his face shining. "And treason is a capital offense..."

"Sir," as first lieutenant, Peter was standing at Walker's elbow. "I was present when this incident occurred," he said, "Hare expressed a sympathy with the Catholic suffragist movement—which is not an illegal nor a treasonous organization."

"He added a great deal more in Irish, sir," said the second lieutenant.

"And the speaking of Irish is an offense in itself," Walker finished with a smile. "Let him have twenty."

"Twenty lashes, sir?" asked the boatswain with a tinge of disappointment.

"Twenty dozen."

Tears leaked from Patrick Hare's tightly closed eyes and ran into his torn mouth as he was tied to the grating.

"Sir," said Kenyon again, "might I remind you that, only last week, Doctor O'Connor said he was not to be punished again for a month, to let his heart recover from the strain."

"O'Connor? Yes, well, he would say that, wouldn't he? These people are as thick as thieves." Walker frowned at the boatswain. "Well? Lay on, man."

"Sir..." there was an unmistakable urgency in Kenyon's

31

tone now. Too much, for at the sound of it the captain's face suffused with red. His lips drew away from his teeth; his eyes disappeared into fleshy slits.

"Do you want to join him, Mr. Kenyon? Well? Do you? The next time you question me, I will have you under the lash, sir, admiral's favorite or not. Do you understand me?"

"I do." Peter bowed his head, and a muscle worked in the angle of his jaw. "I understand you very well," he said in a meek, polite voice that made Walker turn back to his business with a smile. But Summersgill had seen the young man's eyes, alive with fury and a kind of sympathetic fear, and he heard the criticism at the heart of this surrender.

They threw Hare's body over the side along with a boy of thirteen called Joseph Zacharias, guilty of falling asleep on watch, who had been given the choice of starving to death or being thrown out to swim home. He was alive when the sharks got him, but the prevailing opinion was that it was still the better choice.

"I have never seen such a travesty of justice," said Summersgill. In the afternoon, when every spot had been scoured from the decks, the men were below, mending their clothes, and a chill rain had set in above, he had found Peter in the wardroom, head bent over a glass of port as though to veil his betraying eyes from the world. "No wonder the Admiralty have such a difficulty in recruiting enough men. Is it the same throughout the navy?"

"I wonder you ask me, sir." The young man looked up with a glitter of green fury and shame like the sudden sparking of an emerald.

"I ask you because it's clear to me that a bruised face is a small price to pay to be spared the lash. Because I have never for one moment believed that *this* is the career you love so well and write so eloquently about to your poor mother that she simply has to read the letters to all her neighbors."

Kenyon gave a snort that might have been laughter and passed the decanter. "You know, sir," he said quietly, "that I am as recently come to this ship as you are yourself. But that time has been long enough for me to learn that Bates is an awkward, unhandy, ill-tempered rogue." He looked down, drawing a little noose on the table in the ever-present damp. "And that Hare was a good man. Well liked. Ready with a kindness. You understand? I spared the wrong one. I should have found a way to..."

Silence for a moment, and Summersgill wondered how many of the other blank-faced officers suffered so, how many of the boys wept into their pillows every night, mute and hopeless. "*Is* this how the whole navy works? Is this how *you* would run a ship?"

Kenyon looked at him sideways, with a wary look such as Summersgill had never seen on his open face before, then drained his glass and stood. "Would you like to climb to the fighting top, sir? There is a fine view. I can recommend it."

There was not, in fact, a view worthy of the name—gray waves and gray drizzle slanting sideways across the surface of the sea. Water ran down the masts and the rigging about them with a faint, musical trickle, and Summersgill huddled in his borrowed oilskins and felt impressed with himself for climbing to this eminence without a second's fear.

"On the *Northumberland* we used to dance," said Kenyon, who stood with one hand on the shrouds, leaning out into unsupported air. "All the long weeks of sailing with the trade winds—the mids would skylark and the men dance and sing. The officers...we put on a play, with a musical review and poetry readings."

"Not like this."

33

"No." He turned with a flash of sudden intensity. "I'm not saying that we didn't flog. We have the combings of the jails thrust on us to turn into sailors. Dumb, illiterate, violent brutes, who don't understand anything but force. I am no opponent of flogging at need, God knows. But..."

He fell silent again, and Summersgill could see the keen gaze automatically sweep the rigging and deck, whether looking for nautical perfection or for the captain's spies, Summersgill didn't know.

"Do you remember my tutor, Mr. Allenby?" said Kenyon, seemingly at random. "He was a great judge of horses. He used to say that the last thing you want is a hunter so broken that it will only obey. You should hope for loyalty and a spirit to match your own, and to establish a rapport with it, such that—if you fell—it would return for you out of affection. There is no comparison, he said, between the lengths that a friend will go for you and the grudging obedience of a slave." Looking down from the dizzying height into the waves, he said, "I have often thought the world would do well to heed his wisdom."

"Is a ship much like a horse?" Summersgill asked, amused by the realization that this was the answer to his question. He had not yet caught the young man openly saying anything seditious. Not even critical. But such innocent lying, such half-hearted concealment of the truth beneath so obvious a metaphor! Poor Peter! He would never make much of a conspirator.

"It is like a horse, sir, in the sense that a horse is faster and stronger than a man. Only man's authority over the beast prevents him from being trampled into the dirt every time he applies the whip. In the same way, the *Nimrod* has seven hundred and ninety-three men, and forty-five officers, including the boys. Only our authority and the affection—or terror—in which we are held prevents the men from realizing their own strength. When they trust us and believe in us, all is well. When they don't..."

Summersgill felt for a moment as though the frail platform on which he sat had lurched toward the sea. He had been thinking of Peter's dilemma as a personal one, much like his own—the distress of a reasonable and fastidious gentleman at having to participate in a distasteful system. But there was more than disgust at play here—there was a mortal, abject dread.

The bestial faces of the sailors flashed into his mind, gazing up in silent, powerless hatred at the gold braided figures on the quarterdeck. Suppose their hatred did at last boil over? What example of restraint and kindness had they been set? It didn't bear thinking about.

"Mutiny?"

Kenyon gave him a smile as thin as a garrote. "Indeed. I must therefore do everything in my power to support the present regime. And you had best pray, sir, that the men continue terrified of their captain and in awe of their officers. Because if it ever crossed their minds that he—and we—are only human, I should not give you a farthing for our lives."

Chapter Five

The noise pummeled her, picked her up, swept her away, tossed in the din like a doll in a mill race. Astounding, unbearable, exhilarating. The air stank of fireworks and, mysteriously, Emily wanted to laugh and laugh for the sheer glee of it. Stuffing her hands into her ears, she did so and could not hear her own voice over the thunder.

Above, a ferocious sun was beating down on deck, tar was falling from the yards in sticky rain, and it was tacky underfoot as the caulking between the deck-planks softened. Down here on the gun-deck, that sweltering heat was added to by the bursts of fire, the tons of red-hot brass, and the bodies of three hundred men, their skins shining, sweat falling onto the guns to go up in steam as soon as it touched.

Emily stood beside and a little behind Captain Walker, watching. Now that she had been put in her place and made no attempt to leave it by speaking to him, they had reached this amicable state in which both pretended the other did not exist. The pretense did not allow any familiarities to be taken, however, so just as Walker had made no concession to the weather, so Emily had not permitted herself to do so either, and at times she thought she should fall down simply from the heat. Sweat ran down her back, down her legs, making her petticoats cling suffocatingly beneath the stiffly hooped weight of her gown. Her torso itched, the creases in her shift pressed into her skin by the tight, boned stays, and the sack dress she wore on top felt heavy as armor, so that she could hardly walk or lift her arms. How the gun crews could stand it, she couldn't imagine. At the thought, in sympathy, her joy began to wear off.

These men had been awake half of the night as they trimmed and re-trimmed the sails to squeeze an extra knot of speed out of the ship, trying to make up for the time lost to the storm. They had been on their knees before dawn, scrubbing the decks, pumping up the salt water, scouring the planks with holystones and flogging them dry with bundles of rags. Now they worked like Trojans in an inferno that would undo any man's strength, and faces that had been alight with the glory of the great guns were beginning to look numb and closed with exhaustion.

Outside, boat crews labored to pull rafts of barrels far forward into position to float past as targets, and in the brief break while Walker was scowling at his watch, Emily noticed two of the gun captains surreptitiously debating. Mr. Anderson, tears in his eyes, his pasty white face whiter still with fear, was whispering urgently to Mr. Andrews. As soon as Walker looked up, the child flinched away, shaking his head emphatically.

Finally, Andrews patted Anderson on the shoulder and strode down the awfully bare corridor of planks between the gasping gun crews, Walker's disapproving eye resting on him the whole way.

"You have something to say, mister?"

"Aye, sir. Mr. Anderson feels that number six is dangerously overheated, sir. I've looked at the piece and I concur. The touch-hole is almost white hot."

"And Mr. Anderson did not have the guts to report this himself?"

"Sir, he..."

"Don't think I haven't noticed how you mollycoddle these boys, Andrews." Walker narrowed his eyes and thrust his face forward. In response, Mr. Andrews drew himself up with an unconscious, pugnacious quirk to his mouth. More like one of the wild Irishmen who roamed the streets of St. Giles half-cut and looking for a fight, Emily thought, than like a sober officer of His Majesty's Navy.

Seeing the physical threat failing, Walker changed tactics. "Or is it something else, eh," he asked, raising his eyebrows, "that makes you so tender of the little lads? Well, Mr. Andrews, I hanged a man just the other week for that." Emily watched with interest as the young man's face paled with shock at this, and she wondered what the captain was suggesting. Not... Oh, no, surely not. Oh, that was beyond the pale! What a vile thing to be accused of, no wonder he looked so appalled.

From her own experience with the boys, there wasn't a jot of truth in it, but someone was bound to believe it. Someone was bound to "explain" the offense to the children, and thus pollute their life with one more nightmare. Someone was bound to bump into Mr. Andrews in the dark between decks and give him a beating, just in case. What a vicious man Walker was, and how inventive with his methods of control. Lord, how she did despise him!

"No, until Mr. Anderson grows the balls to make his own decisions, he cannot expect me to listen. Dismissed."

The targets were let loose. The note of the cannon was different as they bellowed—they leaped as they recoiled, the chains that held them to the hull twanging taut, the impact of their weight making the whole frame of the ship shudder. There were worried faces as the crews jumped out of their way, yelling and cursing as men began to burn themselves on the hot metal. In snatched intervals of silence, there was a delicate, metallic pinging noise.

She was just beginning to wonder whether it would be a good time to leave when number six exploded.

The din was staggering. The flame even more so. A wave of incandescent heat washed over her, and a thrumming sound passed her left ear. Her world paused strangely, so that between the explosion and the first scream there seemed a slow, infinite time in which to think but where movement was suspended.

Then someone shoved past her, bucket in hand, and everything resumed its usual pace. She turned to find the deck aflame—a seething chaos of men pouring water, stamping on fire with their bare feet. The crew of number six lay scattered around it, broken and as red as the cannon itself.

Little Anderson was taking the pulse of a man, apparently unaware of the shard, thick as an ax blade, embedded in his own thigh. "Mundy and China George are alive," he cried in a watery voice, struggling to lift the closest man to him—he hadn't the strength to lift the seaman's head and shoulders. "Someone help me! Oh!"

Noticing his own wound, he gazed at it, swaying, before his eyes rolled back and he fell. Andrews made an instinctive movement towards him and stopped, his face grim, before deliberately turning away to lift Mundy onto a hastily improvised stretcher. It was Chips, the ship's carpenter, who knelt by the wounded boy's side, trying to find a place to press on the wound without driving the jagged brass further in. There was a smell of charring flesh. All of the shrapnel was still red hot.

Emily tried to move forward, and only then realized she was shaking so hard she could hardly stand upright. A rage that felt almost like a religious experience overwhelmed her, sweeping her along before it. "He *said,*" she hissed between her teeth, clamping them together between words to still their chattering, "he said it wasn't safe! He said it! Why didn't you listen?"

"Too bloody right, missy!" Suleiman "Sully" Chips looked up with cannon fire in his eyes. He was a slender man with the build of a jockey, whose deep, almost blue-black skin had fascinated Emily on sight. He had been so amused by her regard that he expanded on it at every meeting with a yet more implausible story of his native land.

In this place of oppression and silence, he had been—like Hawkes—one of the few comfortable acquaintances Emily had made, and she thought him too gentle, too good-humored for the life. Now, however, there was nothing gentle about him; the veins stood out in his neck as he hurled himself forward at the captain. He never got close; recognizing the signs of a man pushed too far, he was suddenly surrounded by fellow sailors, trying to calm him down or, failing that, to drown out his accusing voice.

"Chips, leave him be."

"Come back here to the boy; we've to move him."

"Let it go! Sully, let it go!"

But Suleiman would not let it go. He drew himself up to his full height of five-foot-one and in a loud voice demanded, "Aren't none of you *angry*? Han't any of you got the guts the young missy's got? We all fucking know who killed these men. We all know it! Han't any of you the stones to stand up and make it stop?"

"Leave. Now." The second lieutenant came up beside Emily, his hand on his sword, loosening it in its scabbard. At the sight she realized the peril—imagined the gun deck erupting into violence. The officers were armed with swords, and marines were even now filing in behind them with rifles and bayonets in their hands, but the men had cannonballs and cartridges of gunpowder. If it came to a fight, she could vividly imagine the carnage. So close they lived to this avalanche of barbarism. Her glorious anger faded at the thought, and fear replaced it. She shook out her skirts, squeezed between the line of rifles and ran away, feeling cowardly and humiliated and desperately afraid.

Chapter Six

"Are..." After the rigors of punishment day, Walker had retired to his cabin to rest, and Summersgill found Peter Kenyon standing very stiffly on the quarterdeck in the isolation of profound shame. "Are you well?"

He couldn't tell whether the rigid posture was due to pain or to the unbearable affront to his dignity, but he suspected the latter. It was a matter of embarrassment even to himself to acknowledge the atrocity.

Kenyon had observed that some leniency might be possible in the sentencing of Suleiman Chips, "a good man, overcome by a temporary fit of grief", and on hearing Walker sentence him to keelhauling, had objected that keelhauling had been banned by act of parliament some years ago as too barbaric a punishment for naval use.

One could argue that he had known the risk he was taking, speaking up—the captain's warning was unequivocal—but nevertheless not a single man on board had imagined Walker would really go through with his threat. It tore a hole in the laws of nature to suppose an officer and a gentleman could be treated like a common man. The sense of disorientation, of the world gone mad, was more frightening than the punishment itself.

Summersgill himself, not bound by naval tradition, had left the quarterdeck so that he might not see his young friend being flogged like a common tar, and now Kenyon acknowledged that kindness by a slight lift of the lips. "I'm prime, thank you, sir. Yourself?"

"I admit to feeling somewhat oppressed." Summersgill looked down to where the body of Chips lay sewn into a hammock. "Something has to be done," he said. "Must you bear this? Can you not call him out? I swear to God if he had done the same to me, I would!"

Kenyon smiled, as though charmed by the thought of Summersgill dueling. True, he was not the most likely combatant, but there were some insults even the most peaceable of men could not endure. Honor would demand action, even from him.

"The captain would be quite within his rights to refuse a challenge," Kenyon said softly, his voice rough. Frowning at the sound of it, he turned away to watch the sea. His hands were white on the rail, and there was a persistent tremor in the muscles of his arms. "It isn't possible to maintain discipline in a ship where the officers are fighting duels over every trifling slight. We must learn to accept a certain amount of humiliation in the exercise of our duty, so the admiralty says. And if I were to fight him despite a refusal, not only would it be murder, but it could well precipitate the mutiny we fear."

"Would that be such a bad thing?"

Kenyon laughed, ducking his head. The movement concealed his eyes but bared the spreading bloodstain on his collar. Summersgill looked away quickly, as he would from any obscenity.

"It has the potential to be very bad indeed. Yesterday I would have said I could hold the crew together through my own authority." The half hidden smile shaded into bitterness. "But you've seen what has become of that. And the authority of the other officers, with me. If we may be punished like ordinary men, why should we be obeyed like gods?"

"You're saying it wouldn't stop with the captain?"

"Exactly so." Kenyon raised his head. With the sea shining behind him only the small lines of endurance around his mouth distinguished him from the figure of a martial saint painted on a church wall. "I don't think they would kill me at first—the stripes might save me for a few days, until they realized I wasn't going to join them. I don't think they would kill you or your wife..." he sighed, "but it would not surprise me either. They would certainly kill— possibly torment—young Hawkes and his messmates. Anderson, too, if he survives the surgery. And I hope I do not need to mention the fate that would be suffered by your ward and her maid. You have no conception, sir, of what these men are capable of when their blood is up."

Peter shuddered. It was only a small, involuntary flinch, but from a man who faced Walker every day, it spoke volumes. Summersgill thought about Emily and the twelve-year-old "young gentlemen" and felt his throat close with dread. He drew out his handkerchief and pressed it to his lips, forcing himself to breathe in the calming smell of lavender.

"Sir?" said Kenyon, watching as Chips' tie-mate, Boyd, made to shake his fist at the quarterdeck. The coxswain caught the arm, pulled it down, and hurried him away, pressing a packet of tobacco into his hands. "If I can keep the crew together until we strike soundings in St. George, can you get the captain removed once we arrive?"

"I think I can!" Summersgill had not been thinking so far ahead, but now he thought about Admirals Sullivan and DeBourne who both had sons involved in minor smuggling activities. They would undoubtedly prefer the young men to be gently warned rather than prosecuted. "Yes, yes, almost certainly. If I write the letters today I can have him diverted into a career in the dockyards within a quarter...or perhaps better say a half year."

Kenyon laughed again—a bark of appalled dismay. "Half a year! We will be lucky if there's a week's tolerance left in the men"

He made an abortive movement as if to reach out and take Summersgill's arm, and though his face was as composed as always, Summersgill had known him from childhood and discerned both an apology and a request for reassurance. The second touched him deeply. Such a splendid young man to be looking to him for help, and yet so young. So young to be bearing this burden.

"I hope you will forgive me, sir, if I say that my greatest concern is not our lives at all. We were sent to Bermuda to combat privateers, and the *Nimrod* is a floating fortress. There isn't a settlement on the islands or another ship in these waters could stand against her."

"That is a pleasing thought, surely?"

"It is. As long as she remains in the navy. But once the men are branded mutineers, then what? They'll have this ship and nothing to lose. I dread to think of the damage they could wreak with it."

Summersgill pictured it. Bad enough the fleets of cutters, sloops, and brigs that flitted from isle to isle making it impossible for decent folk to live without fear of robbery or violence, but add the *Nimrod* and you would add terror. "Oh, I agree!" he said, appalled, "I agree. But what can we do?"

Kenyon gave him a smile of exceptional sweetness. "If the men do mutiny, and I can get down there myself, I intend to blow the powder magazine."

Summersgill wondered suddenly why he had taken this position. He was a landed gentleman and a mathematician, not an adventurer. The realm of sudden death and glory had never appealed, not even when he was young.

"However," Kenyon continued, "it's more likely that the men will get the officers out of the way first, and if I can't..."

Heroism at his age? His skin shrinking away from the vision of himself setting a candle flame to hundreds of tons of gunpowder, Summersgill swallowed. Would there be time for it to hurt? Time to feel the scalding flame, as though he swam in molten lead? Did his oath of allegiance absolutely require that? And if it did, would he really have the courage to go through with it?

Yet could he continue to live, knowing himself a coward? Hadn't he said himself that sometimes honor demanded action? Well. Well, why not?

"My family?" he said, fighting a need to weep at the thought of them, alone in this harsh world, alone on the treacherous sea. "Promise me you will put them into a boat. Promise me my wife and daughter will live."

Glancing aft, Kenyon's eyes lit on the group of midshipmen who were heaving the log to determine the ship's speed, unnaturally studious and quiet for such young boys, their faces pinched with fear. "I mean to take Andrews into my confidence and give him the job of making sure all the youngsters get aboard the longboat. Bess should go, too, this will be no place for her."

He looked back with a rueful smile. "I would certainly have asked you to go and him to stay," he explained, "if it weren't—you understand I mean no disrespect—for the fact that he is a better navigator and a better sailor than you, and so stands a better chance of bringing them safe to shore."

Unexpectedly, Summersgill found himself laughing. "Had I had known the advantage of having such a trade I might not have taken so great a care to remain entirely ignorant all my life." He took Kenyon's hand and shook it, resigned. "Very well, Peter, should it become necessary to blow us all to kingdom come, you may count on me."

Chapter Seven

"I think I can brush the stains from the inside of my coat. But the shirt is ruined." Kenyon twisted the linen as though he was wringing a neck. The pressure squeezed out a trickle of blood that dripped onto the clean floor of their cabin. "My best shirt only fit for handkerchiefs, God damn him!"

Josh drew his gaze back to the dark mirror of his wine with a sense of pressing danger. The *Nimrod* had never been a happy ship, but it seemed to him that some special malevolence lay on this voyage. He could feel himself surrendering to it, growing listless, reckless, and this last blow had left him reeling. He had not thought it was possible to hate Walker more, but this... it was unspeakable.

He risked glancing up, meaning to say so, and caught Kenyon's eyes. They were full of fire and fury, hotter by far than his words, and the look of implacable anger made Josh's heart stall in delight. Such beautiful eyes! So fluid, so expressive, so very green in the gold of the lantern.

Control yourself! He should certainly not be leaning forward, gape-mouthed and entranced. Kenyon might notice. He might notice and understand. Then...then it could be Josh, hanging by his neck from the yard arm, slowly choking to death.

"The shirt is not the only thing in ruins." Josh's voice sounded unnaturally loud to himself. Walker had stepped over the line, and now he was just a little too angry to keep his mouth shut. "By God, sir, you might be his latest victim, but you are not his first—you've seen how he treats the men."

"They cannot appease him," Kenyon agreed and tried to lean down to mop the bloodstain away. His hiss of pain was soft and lay unacknowledged between them, for it was a mark of how far their friendship had come that he let himself flinch at all—a human weakness he would not have shown to another soul on board. "They run about furiously to look active but achieve nothing. I believe he's afraid of them. But the more he tries to grind them down, the more just cause he has to be afraid."

He's afraid? Josh had never thought of it like that. He had imagined Walker merely loved the power. But if he was only a small, terrified man trying to protect himself from those he believed were stronger than him, did he then deserve pity? *No, I think not.*

Kenyon shuffled gingerly forward to the edge of his cot and braced himself to slip off, so that he could kneel and clean the floor without bending. The movement took him from deep shadow into lamplight, baring his shirtless skin to Josh's rapt gaze. Mother of God! Such arms he had, pale and strong, the yellow light pooling in their curves. His long neck and flanks and chest were sleek as cream and scarcely scarred. And his back, the elegant curve of spine brutally cut from waist to shoulders, swollen, bruised, and oozing blood.

Josh made a noise, clapped his hands over his mouth to stifle it, and cursed his vivid imagination. It had chosen that moment to replay to him the scene of punishment on deck; the beautiful young man tied to the grating, the lash, Kenyon's frown of pained concentration, the grunts of impact and the small, involuntary gasps of his breathing.

I was appalled, I was! Oh Mary and Joseph! Why must I be such a monster?

"Are you quite well?" Kenyon looked up with terrible

innocence. Oblivious.

"Just feel...a little sick." Josh drained his wineglass, filled it up again and drank half down before he felt collected enough to go on. "It looks painful. For all love, sir, lie down. I'll swab the floor."

The lieutenant retreated, easing himself down to lie on his stomach with his head propped on one arm. That was better, for now only his amused expression met the light, and even that was half-hidden behind the veil of his long, dark hair. "I made the mess; I should clean it," he said. Josh's mother had had a similar saying, and the familiarity of it was a balm after that rush of paralyzing lust. Affection was safer.

"I know my place," he said, smiling and had begun to relax over scouring the stain away, when the treacherous voice in his head added, *On my knees for you.* He choked again and scrambled back to his bottle. It was a difficult game he played with the wine—he needed it to knock himself out so that he neither lay awake listening to Kenyon breathing nor ran the risk of speaking out of his extraordinarily vivid dreams. But he paid in evenings of lowered inhibitions, the mortal dread of exposure, and lately a growing suicidal wish to confess all, to let the older man know what he really felt. Only the knowledge that it would be playing into Walker's hands held him back, barely.

"I wonder if you do."

"Beg pardon?"

"Is it the drink?" Kenyon watched him with a measuring, alert gaze that—to Josh's muzzy thoughts at least—seemed gentler than any he had used before. "You seem seaman-like and efficient to me, bright enough, able to charm or daunt the men at will, and well able to command. What keeps you from passing for lieutenant? You cannot *want* to be a midshipman all your life."

"On this ship? You, if anyone, should know what it's like by now. I only wish I'd never been made acting lieutenant at all. It was that that made him notice me, and God knows how it'll end." He found the words pouring from him in a kind of ecstasy of relief. Years, it seemed, he had yearned for someone to say these things to, and to find that confidant in Kenyon was almost too good to be true. "I'm not totally without ambition. Were I out of his reach I'd qualify tomorrow, but that isn't going to happen now, is it? So I wish I had damn well kept my head down and stayed unobserved and unimportant 'til I died."

Their shared anger and the honesty felt more intoxicating than the wine.

"It is a far worse pain than the stripes to me," said Kenyon softly into the private, swaying gloom, "to see so many excellent things go to waste. This is a beautiful ship, yet he makes her feel like a prison transport. In the right hands, this crew could be the equal of any in the fleet—and he treats them like dumb brutes, officers and men alike. And you... There are times I see a fine spirit in you, a fighting spirit. Then, of a sudden, it fails. Has he broken you, too? Is there nothing left that can be salvaged?"

"Are you calling me excellent?" Anger Josh understood and could navigate, but praise made him stop short, disbelieving and a little anguished. In drink, the thought of being called "excellent" made him want to weep, though sober he might have appreciated its irony. *You would not think so, sir, if you knew what I wanted to do to you; what I wanted you to do to me.*

"I am." Kenyon looked at him with an open expression, almost nervously. There was a silence, and Josh's heart beat against his throat like the wings of a bird. No one—starting with his mother—had ever thought him worth such praise. Even to God, whose loving kindness was supposedly infinite, Josh was nothing but an abomination to be wiped from the face of the earth with brimstone and fire. He was used to disdain, but he didn't know what to do when faced with kindness. Taking in a harsh breath, he turned his face to the screen to conceal the threat of tears.

Conscious that he had strayed too far on delicate territory, Kenyon hitched himself up to take another long drink of the several pints of rum which had been pressed on him in sympathy by the men and changed the subject. "I have been hoping to uphold the present regime at least long enough for us to reach our destination, but now I wonder. Could I call him out?" His face hardened again. "Summersgill practically suggested it. He'd back me if I chose to, I think."

"Challenge Captain Walker to a duel on his own quarterdeck?" Josh repeated, his spirit thrilling at this audacity.

"On land it would wear well enough. The world understands that a gentleman cannot be expected to bear such an insult."

Did Josh really need to point out the hopelessness of this plan? The absolute authority of a naval captain that superseded any moral law? "But we're not on land."

"No... No." Kenyon tried to turn over onto his side, but clearly his injuries had begun to stiffen, the bruises to bloom and the cuts to tighten, because he gave a startled hiss and lay back down, frowning wearily at the floor. "Some other reason would have to be concocted, and then I should need to be convinced that every man on board would be prepared to swear to the lie."

This time the silence was one of enormity. Josh's glass rang twice as he put it down, betraying the tremble in his hand. Swinging his legs over the edge of his cot, he let himself be seen, partly dressed and frightened as he was. "Isn't that...*mutiny*?"

Kenyon smiled. It was, perhaps, the sweetest expression Josh had ever seen on a man's face, with its perfect mixture of vulnerability and amusement, resignation and entreaty. "If I place my life in your hands," he said softly, "it is because I know it's safe there."

If Josh had been fragile before, these words shattered him. For a moment he forgot how to breathe, how to think, as the storm overtook him, and he ran helpless before the swell of agony and denial. The words were out of his mouth before he had time to consider or regret. "You would not be so quick to trust me if you knew what I was."

"What you are?" The gaze became quizzical, still light-hearted on the surface, but colored with shades of compassion and concern beneath. "I don't...I don't know what you mean."

"If I place my life in *your* hands, will it be safe there?"

"To the utmost of my strength."

Josh took a breath and tried to say it; "I...I.." His heart stuttered as wildly as his words, choking him. He looked at the wall, the floor, the lantern—they glared back, implacable, refusing to help. *I will hang for mutiny or die at the hands of the crew.* It made it easier to force himself out of the cot to crawl on hands and knees across the tiny space, the gulf which was all that separated him from that smile. *If I'm going to be killed anyway...*

Reaching out, he pushed his fingers into the thick darkness of Kenyon's hair, the sensation pounding over him, drowning him. Stroking the errant locks out of the lieutenant's face, he leaned down and touched his lips to the corner of a mouth that had opened a little in surprise. Flushed skin and sweat, and Kenyon licked his lips—perhaps nervously—but at the tiny flickering touch Josh couldn't help himself. Both hands twisted wrist deep into that glorious hair—*soft, so soft*—and he lifted the older man's face to his own, claimed the mouth full on, plunging deep, luxuriating in the taste and the firmness and *Peter, oh, Peter. Oh, God, Peter!*

Something breaking in his chest—his heart, probably—forced him away, forced him to huddle miserably in the middle of the deck with tears spilling onto his cheeks, waiting for the recoil, waiting to be punched and shunned.

He didn't fear death, for the lieutenant was a man of his word, but Josh was basely, burningly ashamed. *And if he hates me...* He wiped his eyes on his sleeves, looked up— best to know the worst at once—and was met by a look of plain astonishment, almost wonder.

"Ah," said Kenyon uncertainly.

Was he blushing? He was! Actually blushing, shy as a maiden. "I...didn't know."

"Are you not going to run to the captain and tell him you've discovered a threat to the ship?" Though his voice was thin and bitter as Tuesday's soup, Josh was proud of himself for being able to speak at all. He had kissed the first lieutenant; no one could ever again say he lacked nerve.

Kenyon shrugged, and the movement must have jostled his back because he went suddenly white and silent, his muscles standing out beneath the skin as he tensed against the pain. Without thinking, Josh reached out to stroke his hair again for comfort. Amazingly, rather than curse and knock the hand away, Kenyon closed his eyes at the touch and slowly relaxed The smile returned, tentative, unsure and all the more charming for it. "Should I?"

Of course you should. "I'd rather you didn't."

"Well, then."

Such mercy was inconceivable. Josh prodded at it, waiting for it to turn into something more familiar. The demand that he get out of the lieutenant's sight before his skinny neck was wrung, for example. "You still think I'm not...I'm not utterly worthless?"

"I still think you are excellent and admirable," said Kenyon. By now he had surrendered so completely to the repeated caress—and the rum and his injuries—that he was sprawled like sand over the thin mattress, his voice slipping towards sleep, heavy and soft. "And as I'd rather neither of us were hanged, whether for mutiny or anything else, I'll try to hold the crew together until we reach Bermuda."

With evident effort, he opened one eye. "Should that not

be possible, I entrust the women and the boys to your care. Get them out of here before the men can lay hands on them. But if the worst does not happen, and we reach Bermuda, I'm to be made commander of a sloop there. If it doesn't distress you to accept the patronage of a mere lieutenant, I will take you with me."

"Distress me?" The foolish laughter came crawling up Josh's throat, throttling him, breaking his ribs. He smothered it behind his hand and snorted, unwilling to shake Peter out of his desperately needed rest. *Did you not notice that I offered you my life? Did I not make it plain that you owned me? You may cause me as much distress as you like, and I will still be yours.* "I would be inexpressibly obliged."

"May we talk later? I'm a bit...tired."

"Whatever you like, sir," said Josh, still finding it hard to believe he was not now in irons. He hitched himself a little closer, so he could lean his shoulder against the cot's wooden side and sit there like a guard dog, watching while his friend fell asleep. "If you want to pretend in the morning that it never happened at all, I'll understand."

Kenyon, he thought, as his breathing calmed in sympathy with the lieutenant's, and he admired the way sleep restored a boyish softness to that stern face, must have known men of Josh's sort before. Nothing else could explain this reaction. He must have had cause to learn they were not all vile, time to come to terms with the thought. Had he not, he would not have been able to slumber at ease in the same room with one, afraid the taint might spread or his virtue be assaulted, or that God's wrath might strike him down for mere proximity.

As the shame fell away, taking the mad hilarity with it, Josh wondered who it had been, the person for whose sake Peter had won this composure. Not a lover—for there had been no recognition and little response to his kiss—but clearly someone he trusted. Someone he thought well of,

53

who had perhaps soothed him to sleep in his youth, making Josh's touch seem expected and familiar. A beloved elder brother? A tutor? If allowed to reopen the subject, Josh would ask.

Leaning across, he snagged his drink and sipped it, becoming aware of the *Nimrod* around him, the tremble of her decks, the comfortable small creaks of her timbers. His mouth was full of the taste of Peter, and he resented the wine for displacing it, even as he edged slightly closer to feel the warmth of the sleeping man on his cheek.

His hands still shook, and small tremblings raced through his body, the aftermath of terror. He wished he could thank God, thank someone, whatever kindly force had taken the moment he had dreaded for a month and turned it into something luminous and beautiful. But he doubted that God would appreciate his thanks on this subject.

Instead he thought carefully, trying not to let the bittersweet hope rise to his head, that while there may have been no response to his kiss, neither had there been any disgust. And if Kenyon was a man made for women—as it seemed—he was also just a man. After months at sea, even he might be prepared to put up with a willing, nay an *ardent* second best. *I would sell my soul if he would only kiss me in return,* Josh smirked at his own drama. *Though that might be because it's worth so very little as it stands.*

But that was the future. More likely when Kenyon woke he would come to his senses, put Josh aside with dismay and move on. Even if he did not, it was likelier that they would both die in an uprising of the crew than that they would survive together long enough for starvation to make him seem an acceptable prospect to Peter.

No, he should stop tormenting himself with faint hopes and just bask in this moment of honest peace. This one night, when he was permitted to stop pretending, allowed to sit in lamp-lit vigil over Peter's troubled sleep and prove the "authorities" wrong. For if he *was* a monster—if he was—

he was now certain he was a monster who could love.

Chapter Eight

Summersgill woke in the darkness and clutched the sheets to his chest. Outside the stern window a gibbous moon was turning the waves the color of bone. Stars shone in a sky cloudless from horizon to horizon, yet thunder was shaking the ship. A deep, menacing rumble encompassed him. When he swung out of bed he could feel it rise through the soles of his feet and invade his bones, as though the *Nimrod* herself were growling.

"Father?"

Emily, too, was awake, her eyes twin gleams of dread in the darkness. He wondered if he looked just as frightened as she and guessed that he did. There was something primal and threatening about the noise, like the howling of wolves.

Was this the moment? He pulled on his clothes and opened the door a cautious crack. At once he was aware there were voices in the noise, voices muttering, cursing in imaginative whispers. Deep voices and the trundle and groan of the thirty-two pound cannon balls being rolled about the decks in a sailors' version of the savages' war dance. The threat and the dread of it took his breath.

Summersgill turned, closed the door behind him and leaned on it, panting, discovering that courage was easier by daylight. He really didn't want to do this. He didn't want to go out of this room at all, among those fiends, sneaking, possibly fighting his way down to certain death.

"Father, what is it?"

Not quite able to look her in the eye, he essayed an unconvincing smile. One breath at a time, one step at a time, he crossed the room, reached out, closed his fingers on the tinderbox and slipped it into his pocket, where it hung remarkably heavy for such a small thing. His wants and desires had nothing to do with it, after all. He had given his word. That was all that mattered.

"Put on your warmest clothes, Emily. I want you to wake my wife and Bess, and tell them to make ready. Take the money and papers from the strongbox, and watch the ship's launch. If you see the young gentlemen getting into it, you are to go with them. They will be expecting you."

She was an intelligent young woman, and he could see that she understood. He blessed her again for her cool-headedness in a crisis. She would need it to control his wife who, though a wonderful woman, was inclined to fits of nerves. "Yes, sir. But, sir…Father. Are you not coming, too?"

The sound that came out of his throat was somewhere between hysterical laughter and sobbing, he swiftly choked it back into a more normal chuckle, so as not to alarm her. "I have my duty to do, my dear. I don't think that will be possible."

This was no way to go to one's death. There should be a ceremony. He set his wig straight, pulled up his stockings and carefully tightened the garters to keep them smooth. Then he pinned an emerald stickpin into his cravat, affixed the heavy gold brooch of the Order of the Garter to the brim of his hat and placed it on his head. That did feel better.

Sitting beside her on the bed, he hugged his daughter, her arms around his neck and the soft cheek against his ineffably beautiful. She was, thank God, capable enough to survive without protection, to use his savings to set herself up in a small shop in Bermuda. A milliner's, perhaps, like her mother's. It was not what he had wanted for his only child, but it was better than what she would get if she stayed here. "Well," he said, "well, you're a brave, good girl, and you must know that I value you immensely. But I'd better cut along now, or it'll be too late. Mind you do as I say, and get in that boat!"

Outside the cabin, he paused for a second, blinded with tears. The tone of the sailors' muttering had changed. A crack, a thud, and a laugh. Summersgill raised his head sharply to see the second lieutenant, Sanderson, scrambling to his feet. The man seemed unable to bear weight on his right ankle—one of the rolling cannonballs must have clipped him "by accident" —and now, unable to walk, he stood shaking with fear and pain, helpless. Summersgill could hear the sailors debating whether to break the other leg or pound him into a pulp and heave him overboard. "No one'd know," Bates laughed again, "and it'd be one less of the bastards to deal with later."

"Shut up, cully! The fucking lubber's watching!"

Summersgill didn't recognize the voice that said this, but at the words he felt every head swivel and every eye affix itself on him. For a moment he stood rapt in terror, as a tiger's prey feels before its glowing gaze. Death by fire seemed quicker, cleaner, infinitely more desirable than the thought of whatever these men might do to him, and his knees shook. With a great effort of will he locked them, stood tall, and smiled. At any moment, at any moment now, someone was going to shout "Get him!"

The voice, when it came, stopped his heart, he clutched at the quarterdeck rail to stay upright, and for a second of abject fear, he did not register that the words were "Sail ho!" shouted by the lookouts at fore and mizzen masts together.

Movement around the edges of the crowd—men fading away into the darkness. Young Hawkes darted out of concealment, where he had been cowering behind the capstan, and ran to the captain's cabin. The hard core of mutineers, Boyd and Bates among them, tried to call men back, but others were already returning the shot to the shot garlands.

A far off thump of cannon and the cloudless night was stained pink. Jets of fire outlined two ships, sails flapping in the billowing smoke, hulls outlined in flashes of gunpowder, only to vanish again when the guns fell silent.

"Beat to quarters!" Hawkes' shrill voice broke as he gave the order, and for a moment there was no movement at all on deck as the beginnings of mutiny were checked by the wild, high thrill of excitement in the child's voice. "It's pirates, lads! Pirates! She'll be our first prize of the campaign. All hands clear for action!"

A lantern, kicked over on the far off brig, kindled her ratlines. Her sails went up in curtains of fire and the unstayed masts drooped towards each other. The second, larger sloop had now seen the *Nimrod* coming like an avenging angel out of the darkness, and her flame-lit sides were thick with men cutting the cables, hauling back the boarding ladders that held them to their prey.

"Bow chasers, fire on the up roll, I want them stopped, not sunk!" Walker was on deck—quite a different man from the spit and polish tyrant Summersgill had come to know, roused from his bed and ready to fight. There was a sort of glory about him, as there had been at times on punishment day—the glow of a man in his element, completely fearless and at ease.

"Riflemen to the tops! Take in sail! Port your helm!"

Marines came thundering up every hatchway, sharpshooters swarming up the shrouds. Insensibly, the feeling had shifted and now men were running to their places, with no more thought than a leaf shows, opening to the sun.

"Lay aloft to furl royals! Lay out and stop flying jib! Man topgallant clewlines, buntlines, and weather braces. Jib downhaul!"

Officers had begun to reappear. The *Nimrod* slowed, turning side-on to the privateer ship. With a great clash, the gun-port covers flew open and the cannons rolled out. The bow chasers were already barking in harsh voices, each shot sent on its way by an enormous jet of crimson flame and a plume of sulfurous smoke. Summersgill could see the black pocks appear in the privateer's white sails where shot had punctured them, and as he looked, the main topgallant yard cracked and fell on the heads of the men trying to scramble back onboard. He felt almost giddy with the reprieve. Not yet dead, not quite yet.

"Back into the cabin, sir, please, and stay there." Peter appeared at his elbow, moving with a fluidity that he would surely pay dearly for when the excitement was over. He, too, was in a state of high exaltation. Throughout the waist of the ship, where the lighter twelve-pounders were beginning to come to bear on the pirates, he noticed something of the same displeasing joy resting upon every crewman. For the first time in the voyage, there were universal smiles. Not the sort of smile one would like to see in one's last moments of life, but smiles nevertheless.

"I...ah..." he said rather lamely and drew the tinderbox out of his pocket.

Peter's eyes widened, and his sharp face softened with a look of enormous respect, but he only bowed his head and took a key from around his neck, where it had hung on a bloodstained cord. He passed it over with a smile, and Summersgill received it as the gesture of friendship it was. For a moment neither of them knew what to say. Then a ball cracked against the bow of the ship, oaken splinters hummed into the netting like angry wasps, and Kenyon remembered himself.

"As long as the cannon are in use, you will never get to the powder room," he said. On deck the sergeant at arms had opened a great chest and was passing out hatchets and cutlasses to eager hands. Boarding parties were assembling;

the captain leading one himself, the third lieutenant another.

"The crisis will come when this is over," said Kenyon, dancing on his feet in his eagerness to get to his own. "These half-trained scum are nothing, but now we have armed our own people. Getting them to hand the weapons back after...? That may be your moment."

"I understand," said Summersgill and shook Peter's hand. "I'll be ready. Well, good luck, lieutenant."

"Thank you, sir. And to you."

Chapter Nine

In the cabin, with the doors open a crack, Summersgill could see down into the waist of the pirate ship, see Kenyon fighting with a furious, economical style. Beside him, Andrews was trying to pull his sword from the backbone of a man. It had wedged fast, and he dropped it, picking up the sailor's blood-slippery cutlass in its stead, his hands the same color as his hair in the light of the burning sail.

Where the fighting was thickest, Summersgill made out Captain Walker, and for the first time in the voyage, he felt a glimmer of admiration. Watching Walker fight recalled bear baiting—the privateers flung themselves at him like a pack of dogs, and he swiped them away like a bear. Laughing, sword in one hand, crowbar in the other, Walker was awful yet splendid, Summersgill thought and yelped, starting forward in shock.

Walker had been back-to-back with Bates, protecting each other, but as Summersgill watched, Bates turned, drew a reefing knife from his belt and drove it hard between Walker's ribs. The captain gasped, stumbled, and went down. Bates smiled with satisfaction, looked up, and saw Summersgill watching him. A jolt of connection, of panic, of paralysis, then Bates turned to defend himself from a blow, and Summersgill closed the door, latched it, and rested his forehead on the glass, wondering if he was about to be sick.

Convenient, he thought shakily. He had a strange urge to laugh, *and no more than fair, after all*. But his legs quaked and his breath would not stop juddering in reaction. It was hard to understand why he felt so overcome—hadn't he practically suggested that Kenyon should do the same? Yet it was one thing to believe in poetic justice, quite another to see it.

Seeing him upset, Emily came to his side and took his hand as she looked out. Pulling her back, he closed the door again, shielding her from the horror that was the realm of men. Sometimes he wished he did not have to deal with it himself, not only because of its barbarity but also because of its reluctant echo in his own nature. For now that the shock was wearing off, his natural cynicism reasserted itself. Bates' actions were appalling, yes. Abhorrent. Yet also tremendously welcome.

A thud of men's feet hitting the deck, voices outside, and Summersgill tucked his hand in his pocket closing his fingers tight on the tinder box. Just in case. "Remember the boat, Emily," he said as he eased open the door once more. "I hope it won't be necessary, but it's as well to be sure."

The slice of open door revealed the *Nimrod's* own people, milling in the waist, their hands tight on their arsenal of weapons. There was a growing ugliness, a tendency to push at any man whose blue coat marked him as an officer. The third lieutenant narrowly avoided being tripped and trampled, and Summersgill set his teeth in his lower lip, sure that Bates had waited too long to act, and nothing less than the slaughter of everyone in charge would now satisfy the crew.

Coming aboard with several of the midshipmen and younger officers ranged about him like a bodyguard, Kenyon paused at the sight of this milling disorder. A flash of concern and thought went through his eyes, then he set his followers aside and walked confidently through the press of men to the quarterdeck ladder. Standing on the first step, head and shoulders above the crowd, he called out, "Men, I regret to have to tell you Captain Walker is badly injured and may not live."

A strange reaction went through the sailors, part doubt, part superstitious dread. Then someone at the back of the crowd cheered, and there was sparse scattered laughter.

A detachment of marines came over the side. Behind them, Summersgill made out Andrews unobtrusively attaching the ship's longboat to the winch, some of the boys lifting a barrel of water into its stern. They, too, believed this was the moment, then.

Certain that the mere sound of it would disrupt the fragile truce, Summersgill forced himself to breathe in and out once. The whole ship was tensed like the trigger of a pistol, drawn back almost to the firing point. He breathed again and resented the need, frightened to move.

In the strained silence, Kenyon took off his coat. During the fighting, the stripes on his back had begun to bleed again, and his shirt was marked with long, red parallel lines. *A deliberate display?* Or an instinctive act of solidarity with Walker's other victims?

Whichever it was, the crew responded. Faces that had been implacable creased with confusion as a frisson of fellow-feeling went through the Nimrods.

"For the time being, this places me in charge. Lt. Smith, the prize is yours; pick your prize crew and get aboard her immediately."

"Yes, sir." Smith nodded. Fear made his face bone white, but his voice held the genuine quarterdeck bark as he singled out a number of men. They looked at one another for support, for signs of defiance, but none seemed willing to make the first move, and Smith's shoulders relaxed a fraction as the sailors came to his side.

"You will be glad to hear, gentlemen," Kenyon continued, "that the vessel we rescued has promised a bounty for every man as soon as we get to port, and that's on top of the prize money for the sloop. A good night's work. As there will be considerable labor tomorrow, swaying up replacement masts on the prize, we will splice the mainbrace tonight."

More cheers, and this time the laughter rang less hollow. Seizing the moment, the sergeant at arms and his mates began to quietly go among the men and hold out their hands for the weapons. Slowly the sailors handed them over, and as the purser brought out the grog they began, one by one, to form themselves into a well worn, comfortable queue.

"The force of habit is a wonderful thing," Summersgill said as Peter made his way up the rest of the risers onto the quarterdeck. They stood for a while side by side, both hanging onto the rail for dear life, neither remarking on it, as the ship eased back into normal life around them.

"Indeed."

"What made you think of..." even now the taboo was so great that he couldn't get the words out; he settled for gesturing at the shirt, shamefully stained and on display.

Bowing his head, Peter gave a wan smile to the deck just in front of his feet. "I've had more rum pressed on me in sympathy this last night than I could drink in a lifetime," he said. "It occurred to me that if the men were sick of authority, an appeal to our common humanity might be in order. We are all Nimrods, after all. One ship's company, in this together."

Nevertheless, Summersgill thought, it must have hurt, to stand there so exposed and to know that he was asking for pity. Indeed, he looked half dead—his color waxy pale, his movements stiffening and growing jerky with pain. "Well," Summersgill found himself automatically lapsing into his fatherly tone of voice, "I dare say it will all look better after a good night's sleep."

"I'm sure it will. I'll have the opportunity to find out when we get to shore. Until then—having only just coaxed the reins into my hands—I dare not put them down again for anything so trivial as sleep."

He knew his own capabilities best, perhaps, but to Summersgill's eyes he seemed sapped to the point of collapse. Worn, even fragile. But then he said, "The captain's injury..." Wincing, he shook his head, "I shouldn't ask, but..." And Summersgill realized this was not merely physical exhaustion but a deeper wound, a strike at the heart of his certainties.

"It was Bates," Summersgill confirmed quietly.

Rubbing his eyes as if to smooth out the involuntary grimace, Kenyon tensed. "You saw?"

At Summersgill's nod, he clenched his jaw, the muscles standing out in his lean face, as the shadows shifted beneath cheekbones and brow. In the east the sky was lightening, and the sound of the ship's bell rang out sweet and regular as though nothing had ever been wrong in the world, but the darkness lingered in Peter's eyes. "Damn!" He walked away, paced back, "Damn!" and caught hold of Hawkes by the shoulder. The boy squeaked, surprised.

"Find Billy Bates, give him my compliments, and ask him to wait upon me *now* please."

Extraordinarily, Summersgill felt the stool-pigeon's stab of guilt. "You can't mean to punish him for it, surely?"

Fragile was not the word for the look Kenyon turned on him then, ablaze with indignation. With all that fervor behind it, it was a pure expression but frightening for all that. "What else can I do? Am I to call him into the cabin and say 'You stabbed the captain in the back, well done, just don't make a habit of it'? For God's sake!"

"Please don't take that tone with me, Peter."

Shying from the rebuke, Kenyon took off his hat and smoothed back sticky, tangled hair. "My apologies, sir. But surely you see that I *must* punish him. I cannot wink at attempted murder. Indeed, for all I know it may be actual murder by now. It is touch and go whether the man survives. And he is the *captain*!"

With a sinking feeling, Summersgill realized there were disadvantages to Peter's certainties. How easily the viewing of the world in absolutes lent itself to injustice, men, after all, being more complicated than the law.

"You would have killed him yourself had he accepted a challenge," Summersgill said and waved aside the protest that that was a completely different thing. "Besides, do you think the crew would stand for it? I should imagine they would declare Bates a hero and hang us, rather than let us harm him. Is this the time for an investigation? Can we not at least put it off until we reach land?"

Peter turned aside for a moment, and the captain's steward, who had been hovering nervously in the background for some time, took this opportunity to bring him a bowl of warm water and a towel. Peter washed the blood from his hands and face, shrugged into the clean coat that was offered, and turned back looking paler yet but a great deal more civilized. For a moment he seemed utterly lost before covering it by glancing up imperiously and saying, "Where *is* that boy?"

"Here, sir!" Hawkes bounded up the ladder two steps at a time. The man he brought with him, however, was not Bates but a civilian, who would surely have been twisting his elegant tricorn between his hands had he not had one arm in a sling. His snuff colored coat was fashionably cut and of the best material but had been sadly mauled in the action, and though he had managed to find *a* wig to go before the *Nimrod's* commanding officer, it was clearly not his own. Unruly blond curls escaped in every direction, making him appear more like a dandelion clock than a gentleman, but his face was grave enough to instantly dash the comic effect.

"Adam Robinson, sir. Master of the *Clara Bush*. The vessel you so gallantly rescued...and I know my second has thanked you before. He...um...spoke of it, but I would just…like to say how deeply, *deeply*...”

“Please, Mr. Robinson.” Kenyon looked away, flustered. “It is no more than our duty. But I’m curious to know why, when I sent my young gentleman to find me a foremast jack, he returned with you.” He raised an eyebrow at Hawkes, who responded by standing rigidly to attention and looking very serious indeed.

“If you please, sir, I couldn’t find Bates on board. So I thought maybe he was with one of the cleanup crews. I run through the *Caesar*—that’s the prize, sir—and Mr. Smith told me he weren’t there, so I went on to the *Clara Bush*, sir, and there…”

“And there…I regret to say. I’m terribly…” Robinson successfully crumpled a corner of his tricorn with his left hand, looking almost ready to cry as he struggled for words.

Knowing that this was probably the first time the young merchant had ever faced battle, Summersgill could completely understand his scattered inability to express himself, but the fact that he would have been the same in the young man’s place did not prevent him from drawing unflattering comparisons with the manliness of the officers around him. Even the boys showed more bravery. He was thankful when Walker’s steward returned with a tray of coffee. The pause, to take a cup, to sip and wrap his hand around solid, comforting warmth, worked wonders for Robinson’s composure.

“I regret to say, Captain, that during the battle four of your men came aboard the *Clara Bush*. They said you had asked me to provide them with a boat so that they could go and alert the rest of the fleet.

“It sounded suspicious, but as you were in the thick of the fighting, there was no way to confirm it. And frankly, sir, I was so overcome with gratitude, how could I be carping or ungenerous in return?”

“How long ago?”

“Half an hour, perhaps a little more.”

Kenyon paced away, hands folded behind him. The men had now drunk their grog, and their ranks had thinned as one watch took to their hammocks. The other began the reassuring ritual of sluicing and scrubbing the decks—Summersgill had to move out of the way quickly to make room for a sailor scraping a bible-sized slab of pumice over the spot where he had been standing.

"They'll be hull-down by now, but could be we could still see their sail from the maintop," Hawkes suggested, with the air of a boy trying to impress.

"Indeed, I will have to consider carefully what to do." Kenyon smiled a rare, genial smile. "You'll stay to breakfast, Mr. Robinson? You must tell me what you require in the way of men and equipment for repairs; I should like to be underway to Bermuda within the day."

The galley stoves had been lit; the contented rumble of several hundred men eating hot burgoo filtered up through the floor. Summersgill, who had become inured to the naval habit of eating anything it was humanly possible to digest, tucked in to his roasted porpoise with relish.

Despite the unorthodox bill of fare, the breakfast party was a great success. Hawkes fidgeted at first but was lured into trading comic songs by the other mids. Robinson relaxed into good-humored volubility and began a long recount of the exact steps which had ended with his ship being boarded.

It must have been a full hour into the meal when Kenyon looked up from the breadcrumb plan of battle and caught Andrews' ever attentive eye. "Mr. Andrews, run up to the maintop, would you, and see if you can't see the *Clara Bush*'s launch. I'm afraid that, in the confusion last night, several of our men may have run."

Later, when the party had broken up, and the work of putting up new masts had begun on both sloop and brig, Summersgill stood in the captain's cabin and watched as Kenyon wrote a large, careful "R" by the side of each of the four men's names.

"Well," Summersgill said, "I now know that the bloodcurdling accounts of derring-do that your mother recounts to her fascinated circle of friends while taking tea are not at all the fictions I used to suspect. I congratulate you."

Looking longingly at the brandy bottle that hung above the table in its ingenious barge, rocking in counterpoint to the sea, he added. "And if it is not too wicked of me, may we drink to Captain Walker's recovery being delayed at least until we reach Bermuda?"

Peter filled up a glass and passed it to him. Sun, flowing through the stern windows, cast moving, tawny bronze pools of radiance on the polished wood of the cabin, as it passed through the fine wine. "According to Dr. O'Connor, that is a certainty, sir. Let us drink, instead, to the *Nimrod,* come through this storm unbowed."

A splendid young man, Summersgill thought again. Just such a young man as he would like for his son. He determined not to let the acquaintance return to distant civility once they arrived. It would make him very happy indeed to see his daughter married so well. "To the *Nimrod*," he said, lifting his glass. "And to us."

Peter laughed, a startled, shy sound, barely to be heard over the froth and whisper of the wake. He closed his eyes briefly, utterly failing to mask the light of pleased embarrassment, and drank. "Indeed, sir. To us."

Chapter Ten

Emily walked out of the cabin into a beautiful morning. The *Nimrod* was still silent, but now it seemed a silence of peace. Men smiled at her as she passed. Only a cable length away, the *Caesar* bustled with activity as Lt. Smith oversaw the raising of a new mast. The sun shone on a deck brown with gore, and she could see the tracks of it down the ship's sides, where a tide of blood had run out of the gutters and spouted into the sea. Looking down, she saw the water was still pink. Something floated there and, recoiling, she saw it was a severed arm.

"Oh!" she said and, covering her mouth, half ran to the other side of the ship, where Mr. Robinson already stood, looking as haunted as she felt herself. She stumbled as she approached, and he took her arm in his undamaged hand, supporting her.

"I am quite fallen to pieces," he said, unconsciously grotesque. "You shouldn't have to... No one should have to see this. What a world we live in that men can do this to one another and be proud of it!"

He was wigless, and his fair hair caught the sunlight, surrounding him with a halo of light that brought out the blue of his eyes, and made the gentle, sensitive look in his face seem like a benediction. Emily's nausea eased suddenly, and she smiled, forgetting to twitch her arm out of a grasp that had forgetfully lingered.

"It is dreadful," she agreed with relief. "But would you not say it was necessary? After all, the men who attacked you would hardly have ceased if you had only politely asked them to go away."

The smile changed his whole aspect. Where melancholy he had seemed a little too boyish, smiling he was an Apollo. Her heart skipped a beat at the sunny kindliness of the expression. When it faded she found herself wishing fervently that it would come again.

"No, I suppose they would not. But I walked through the privateer to come on board. The French do not throw their casualties overboard, and the... Oh, God! The piles of carnage...pulped, like fruit." He took his hand abruptly away from her to cover his eyes. "I was too *happy* at the time to register it. But now it returns to me, like a nightmare—a nightmare I cannot tell myself is untrue."

"We throw our dead overboard?" she said, struck with her own companionable horror. "Unnamed? Unburied? Like refuse?"

For a moment they stood together, watching as Mr. Robinson's crew scrubbed at the decks, pink water gushing from the *Clara Bush*'s scuppers, and while the horror and disgust took up half her mind, the other half rejoiced at having found someone she could speak to who seemed to understand.

"Forgive me!" Now he took his hand from his face and offered it to her, smiling again, a smile that began tentative but became radiant when she placed her fingers in his grasp. "Adam Robinson, owner and master of the wreck that you see over there."

"Emily Jones," she said and automatically dropped him a little curtsy, her fingertips tingling and a warmth spreading down her arm and into her belly at his touch. Some sense of defiance prompted her to add, "My mother is a hat maker in London." And she hugged the delight to her as his smile broadened.

72

"Thank goodness!" He bowed so rustically that Emily's new dancing master would have been scandalized. "I thought you were a great personage! I was a little afraid to speak to you at all."

"I'm very glad you did," she said, hardly caring that it was too bold. After a month with only her elderly father and the barely human men of the navy for company, she felt rescued—a child assured that there are civil people in this world after all. "It has been a long voyage, and the company has been somewhat...limited."

He reached up and toyed with the bow of his cravat, and she found herself watching his fingers, appreciating both the elegant shape of them and the ink stains that betrayed him as a tradesman. It occurred to her then that her father was not going to be pleased with her if she chose to encourage this acquaintance, and at that thought, it became clear to her that she very much wanted to.

"You are not one of these young ladies who spends all her time reading in the Naval Gazette then?" he asked with a nervous laugh.

"No indeed!" she said. "I think trade to be the way forward, for the betterment of our nation and the Empire, and once I am on land, I hope never to have to venture to sea again." It was a little forward, perhaps, considering she knew nothing about him other than that she liked his smile, but the scattered parts of bodies even now being consumed by a feeding frenzy of sharks beneath the keel made her conscious of how uncertain life was and how little time there was to waste. "What is it that you specialize in, Mr. Robinson?"

If he was taken aback by her obvious interest, he did not show it, but his smile did falter as he said, "At the moment? Nothing." His fidgeting fingers left the cravat and rose to toy with his hair, pulling it. "I had a cargo of silk and sweetmeats," he elaborated apologetically, "to take to America to trade for furs. But it seems the enemy's cannon

73

punctured the hold, allowing salt water to get among the boxes and bales. My stock is ruined and my ship... Well, they have been pumping all night, and Lt. Kenyon assures me that his men can keep the labor up until we reach Bermuda. So I have not lost everything, but..."

He laughed again, making her realize that his good humor was an act of bravery, more admirable to her than any physical heroism. "But what appeared a miraculous rescue last night, this morning has become somewhat more complicated. And I have... And there is that bonus I swore, in my enthusiasm, to pay to the men of the *Nimrod*—all eight hundred of them. No. Forgive me, Miss Jones. You are speaking to a ruined man. I do not know where I will find the funds to make good my promise."

"They won't expect it, surely? Once you explain?"

Quite unconscious of the impropriety, Adam took her hand again and pressed it as though they were old friends. "I gave my word," he said gently. "But bless you for caring. May I... I know this is forward of me, but may I be permitted to call on you again, once we arrive? You have cheered a morning I thought altogether bleak, and your smile alone would be motive enough for me to move the moon. If you will say yes, then I will count even this disaster fortunate, for your kindness is worth ruin a thousand times over to me."

Emily laughed, a wave of happiness and embarrassment flowing over her at the words. "That is a little too warm, sir," she said, conscious of the blush that heated her cheeks and hoping that it looked becoming. "But do come and visit me. We have taken a little house on Duke of York Street, near St. Peter's, and I have no acquaintances there. I'm sure I shall be very glad to see you indeed."

Chapter Eleven

"She's everything I dreamed, Andrews! She's beautiful, valiant, high spirited..." Kenyon broke off to lay a hand tenderly on the sweating wooden wall and to smile again, aglow with love.

"Her knees are crank, and her bottom is filthy," Josh pointed out, knowing that although this had to be said it wouldn't make the slightest bit of difference. He drew slightly closer because Kenyon in love was a gorgeous thing to behold, and this was a love he could share, a happiness he could return and augment. "But I admit that when they're replaced, and her copper's scraped, she'll be the sweetest little sloop in the fleet. I give you joy of her."

"Give *us* joy rather. I'm not the only one with a new coat."

When they were turned out together into a foreign land, they had decided to take a small set of shared rooms above the King George coffee house. There—comfortable together after the month lodged in a tiny cabin on board the *Nimrod*—they had waited for the ship Kenyon had been promised when he left England.

It had been a thin time, waiting for the *Seahorse* to complete her refit, Kenyon on a lieutenant's half-pay, and Josh on nothing at all. A time when a cup of coffee was a luxury to be shared and a mutton pie cause for great celebration. But for Mr. Summersgill, who invited Peter to dinner weekly, pressing the leftovers on him "to give to the deserving poor", they might have been hungrier still. The new coat—a *lieutenant*'s coat—sat in its magnificent box in the middle of that threadbare existence like a portent. The first outward sign of something Josh had felt inwardly the moment Peter stepped from his carriage—a change in his universe, the rising of a new star.

He had put the uniform on, of course, as soon after his promotion as he might, and walked down the street to admire himself in the reflections of house windows. A real officer, at last! His father might have been proud, had they still been speaking.

"These waters are lousy with French privateers." Kenyon interrupted Josh's reflections, lifting the lantern he carried to examine the hanging knee which supported the deck above his head. This one showed no sign of rot—the oak was silver gray with age and hard as iron. For a moment he was framed against the ribs of the hull, light in his hand, the solid, golden center of an arched, retreating hollowness. *Like an angel in the cathedral,* thought Josh, and then corrected himself, for no angel ever had so thin and cutting a smile or eyes so determined on death. "And now I have the means to deal with them. She's swift enough to equal any cutter. We can chase them down. Where they flee we can hunt them and take them. If we make our fortune from prize money in the process, so much the better."

Kenyon lowered the lantern, picked his way out between the barrels and piles of stored cable. The wide sleeve of his shirt just touched Josh as he brushed past, and at the ghostlike caress Josh smiled. "Indeed. I should like to be able to *wear* my new coat, instead of these second hand slops. Where I'd find the funds to replace it if disaster befell, I have not the slightest idea."

Kenyon paused, taken aback. By slight subtleties his expression changed from bloodthirsty ardor to regret and then to a hesitance Josh couldn't quite interpret. He put the lantern down on a nearby crate with the air of a man buying time to find the right words. "I..." he said, "I am...sensible of the risk you've taken, choosing to throw in your lot with me. I'm aware that all I've succeeded in doing so far is to reduce you to penury, but..."

"Sir, that's not what I was implying at all."

"I know." Peter bowed his head as if he was ashamed of his own smile. "It should still be said. I'm conscious you've trusted me with your career and received only privation in return. But soon I'll have the chance to show that your confidence was not ill placed, and I mean to make the most of that. You shall not regret your belief in me; I swear it."

Instinctively, Josh looked over his shoulder, to where the hatch grating lay in a pillar of faint striped light abaft the mizzen mast. There were no sounds of movement from the deck above, and no feet disturbed the grayish, filtered radiance. The conversation had taken an unexpected turn towards privacy, and he did not wish to be walked in on while he was struggling with the inappropriate joy of these words, or the even more inappropriate things he wanted to say in answer.

"You've already proved that, sir. The absence of a noose around my neck is cause enough for some loyalty, surely?"

"No!" One got used to Peter being still, measured, even stiff, and forgot that he could also swoop into movement like a hawk. Josh found himself seized by both elbows before he'd even registered the beginning of the lunge. "Is that why you follow me? Out of a kind of self-blackmail? Out of fear? I thought..." He swallowed, looking almost sick with nerves. "I thought there was something more."

Josh breathed in—a breath that seemed to take forever, while his heart paused, frightened, above the great abyss of the future. How easily he could ruin the modest happiness he had attained as Peter's friend by misinterpreting, by leaping out unsupported into the pit.

"I thought you wanted to gloss over the incident," Josh said, wiping his hands nervously against the skirts of his coat. Had he missed something? When they came to shore and took lodgings together, they had had a gentle, fearsomely embarrassed conversation about the unfortunate fate of Peter's rather too well beloved tutor, Mr. Allenby, and then nothing. A few days' awkwardness and then friendship returning like a balm. But had he read it wrong?

Had the awkwardness been in fact an inept, unspoken invitation? He fought off hope and guilt together. "Frankly, sir, when you kiss a superior officer without invitation you feel unreasonably fortunate even to be allowed to let the matter drop."

Unexpectedly, Kenyon smirked. "I'll remember that, next time I accost the admiral." And Josh laughed, sure that he could now turn away, hide his flushed face in the shadows and let the moment pass, leaving him on an even keel again.

But Peter had not let go. It would have taken a saint to struggle against the grip of those long fingered, elegant hands—and Josh was no saint. Though elbows did not normally feature prominently in his erotic daydreams, when they were separated from Peter's skin only by a layer of cotton so thin that he could feel the roughness of rope burns, the callous left by a small-sword, he found himself obsessed by them, unable to concentrate on anything else.

"I admit I was a little...taken aback, at the time."

They moved; Peter's hands moved, sliding from elbows to biceps, and Josh had to bite his lip against the rush of illicit pleasure, the maddening desire to take the one step forward that would enable him to press himself against Peter, hot and tight together. God, he shouldn't have thought of that!

"But the more I reflected on the matter, the more I confess I found myself..." Peter's eyes had a trick of holding the light, as the sea will when the sun is bright, and

Josh—oh how he wanted to swim. "Curious."

No protestations of undying love. It was unsettling—it was almost real. "Curious?" Josh managed in a constricted, breathless voice that was as good as an admission of guilt. If Peter had any sensitivity at all, he *must* know how far he was pushing; he must have the sense to back off now, before it was too late.

"As to what you are willing to die for. I should like to know."

There were a number of objections Josh could have made, and he did try. He honestly did. With his blood singing and his mouth gone dry he did say "I...don't wish to...mistake your meaning."

Kenyon's right hand stroked over Josh's shoulder, came to rest on the back of his neck, the thumb moving slightly, raising the hairs on his nape in a shiver of delight. By themselves, his eyes had half closed, his face tilted up in mute offering, primed and waiting. He made a last ditch defense. "I don't want you to do...anything you'd...regret."

And Peter closed the distance between them. They were touching, Josh could feel the planes of that hard chest, was surrounded, invaded by Peter's heat, his scent. Peter was looking down with wide eyes, his own breath coming ragged now, as Josh's fever infected him. "I should like to kiss you," he said, decidedly. "Unless you object?"

Even the man's voice was like being coated in molasses and licked clean. How was anyone supposed to object to that? "Christ no!" Josh leaned in, surrendering. "I mean yes, sir, kiss me. Oh, yes. Yes, *please*!"

I shouldn't be doing this. Peter snaked an arm around Josh's waist, pleased and intrigued by the way even this small touch made his friend's pulse quicken. He could feel the gasped breath fill the chest pressed against his, and it was uncharted waters from now on, with the forbidden lying like a reef beneath the surface—dangerous, exciting.

How different! He had been lucky enough to know two young ladies in his life, and it seemed natural now to gather his partner gently into his arms, to hold back, careful of her frailty, filled with reverence for a lover so small, so easily hurt. But Andrews was over six feet tall and broader across the shoulders than Peter was himself. Nothing soft about him, and delicate only in spirit. *I really should not be doing this.*

But he wanted to. The kiss they'd shared onboard the *Nimrod* had proved another difference. Drunk, faint, and taken by surprise though he had been, he would have needed complete insensibility to miss the fact that Andrews wanted him with a fury.

Both of the ladies Peter had courted had been respectable, and as such they were untainted by lust, accepting his advances out of generosity—pity even. He had always felt vile for imposing on them—a seducer and debaucher of innocent young women whom he had no real intention of marrying; a libertine, a ruiner of lives. With Andrews there would be none of that. No selfishness, no guilt.

He leaned in, barely having to tilt his head, and tentatively touched his lips to Josh's. That...wasn't so bad. Really, it wasn't. The mouth was warm and firm, the lower lip full, yielding, tempting him to bite. Shifting slightly to press closer, he licked it, tasting, and was rewarded with a little whimper that made him feel warm from head to feet. Mmm...yes, nice.

Josh's arms went around him, pulling him close. A strong hand was behind his head, a second splayed against his spine, stroking down. Easily as that, the balance shifted, and it was no longer him kissing Andrews, but Andrews kissing him—with an ardor that quite undid him. No one had ever, ever wanted him this much.

It dawned on Peter that he was no longer in control—the

responsibility had been taken out of his hands. Unless he wished to struggle like a reluctant maiden, it wasn't his fault that the hand had twisted into his hair, the kiss deepened and heated, or that the pressure of a hard thigh between his legs had grown into something rather more than merely nice. It was bizarre to be on the receiving end of a tide of desire he couldn't equal, unnatural to be the one who had to be coaxed, pleased, seduced, but—God!—the relief! The uncomplicated joy of it.

He heard himself make a low rumble of encouragement, almost a moan, and then Andrews was frantically shoving him away, the caressing hands holding him at a distance. Considerably more aroused than he had expected to be, Peter was ready to be angry at being toyed with, but the expression in Andrews' dark eyes was of fear, surfacing out of a deep, stunned bliss.

"Why...?"

"I heard something."

Peter had forgotten he could hang for this. Even now it didn't seem real—what the hell was so wrong about kissing? But Andrews had instincts honed by a life of threat, and he'd neatened his clothes, taken the lantern and walked away before Peter could even stop panting.

Now he, too, heard footsteps, pausing above the hatch. He heard the grating being flung back and a pleasant voice humming "Hearts of Oak" in an offhand baritone mumble. Hastily retying his disheveled hair, Peter pulled the ribbon taut just as the owner of the pleasant voice leaped the final few rungs of the ladder and splashed into the dirty water of the hold. The lantern light showed a rawboned face, sallow from too much sun, a finely powdered wig, and a lieutenant's coat nearly as new as Josh's, but with the creases shaken out. "Captain Kenyon?"

Settled in himself once more, Peter stood and moved into the light. The sallow young man looked him over with light, humorous eyes and said, "Archibald Howe, sir, reporting for duty. The carpenter's crew told me you were down here."

Peter remembered now that Lt. Howe was the officer promised him by Commodore Dalby, laid off the *Asp* with yellow fever and, as the commodore said "a troublesome young person, but the only one we have available". He managed not to smile at the thought that the commodore was right about the troublesomeness, though it would be a long time before "disturbing a superior officer's experiment with buggery" would be a reportable offense.

"You are most welcome aboard, Mr. Howe," he said instead, resigning himself with reasonable grace to the interruption. "Help Andrews with restowing the hold, will you—I want her a little more brought by the bow—and when that's done go down to the dockyard and see if you can charm me any more cable. Hawser weight for preference, but I'll take whatever they've got."

When Peter came out onto the quarterdeck, just after noon, having spent the rest of the morning checking the salt beef, salt pork, salt horse, dried peas, and other non-perishables, he found Andrews and Howe leaning over the railing together, laughing as if they were old friends. The sun seemed to hang in topaz fury all about them, and the rigging made a beautiful black symmetry against the burning sky.

Inland, parrots flew gaudily over the violent green slopes, but Peter found his eye drawn back to Andrews, whose uncovered hair was tawny-copper in the golden light, and whose face was lit up with humorous scorn as he related one of the *Nimrod's* minor scandals to an appreciative audience. A strange complex of emotions filled Peter at the sight—proprietorial pride, aesthetic appreciation, but mostly a satisfaction such as he felt looking at his very own first command. Joy and a determination to prove himself.

Realizing that he was standing in a public place, woolgathering, with a small—probably intimate—smile on his face, he cleared his throat and schooled himself to sternness. "The dockyard, Mr. Howe?"

"At once, sir!"

When Howe had gone down the side, they were alone but for the ply to and fro of small boats from the other men-of-war and the distant hammering and curses of the carpenters, echoing up from the hold. He let the smile return, and received, in exchange, a look of more sweetness than he'd imagined Josh capable of—the man was normally sharp as a barrel of bayonets.

"Eight bells and a little over, Mr. Andrews. Would you join me for dinner?"

"I'd be honored, sir."

Dinner was two cold pork chops, saved from yesterday, and the heel of a loaf which had served for breakfast. A less glowing heart than Josh's might have called it poor fare. At this moment he could not be so ungrateful, for he was in that rare mood when all things are beautiful, and all people agreeable.

Ducking through the doorway of the small "great cabin" of the *Seahorse*, he wondered that he had never seen before how the curve of windows and the white-painted wood made it seem almost insubstantial, floating in a great light above the sea. What would it be at twelve knots with the deck heeled over and the rigging singing like a wind harp— the wake falling away like white wings, and Kenyon, with that predatory look of his, urging her forward, white knuckled?

Or—please, God—at twelve knots, with the timbers resonating to the triumphant note of power, the swell of the sea; Kenyon pinning him down over that table, and making him fly like the ship—intense and fast and alive. Walking out afterwards—bruised and trembling—carrying such a secret. A secret he could smile over and hoard possessively away to share with only one man in the whole world. A pearl of great price he could protect against the hypocritical, murderous mob, which was so tender and forgiving of their own fornication but would happily destroy him for his.

"I have avoided going into debt so far," said Kenyon, leaving his contemplation of the windows to slide one of the chops across the table, the handkerchief it had been wrapped in now serving as a plate, "but this is becoming ridiculous. I must buy plate for the cabin, a certain amount of good food if I'm to invite my officers to dine, and the dockyard is expecting a sweetener for the spare main topmast, if it's not to go to the *Dart*..."

He paused, and his look of preoccupied business became gradually something shyer and less certain. It was astonishing how a face so hard in all its lines could hold such gentleness. The sun, falling unequally on him, brought out the green of one eye, left the other softly hazel, and Josh found himself studying his commanding officer's eyelashes, wondering how soft they would feel against his lips.

"Forgive me. Was that unfeeling? I'm...not sure how to talk to you in these circumstances."

"As you always do, sir," Josh said, puzzled. "I'm your premier—I need to know these things."

"But are we not also..." Peter looked down, embarrassed, and then up again in a gesture of openness that seemed to take a great deal of bravery, "lovers?"

Having grown used to furtive meetings in back rooms with men who would not acknowledge his presence on the street, the word was a full broadside, and Josh was shattered by the impact of it. *Lovers*! Could Kenyon really be innocent enough to apply that term to this...arrangement? Could he conceivably *mean* that he saw no difference between this and the love he might feel for a sweetheart?

84

Was he offering not only his body but his affections? It was too much—too much. It could not be true.

The uncomplicated happiness with which Josh had entered the cabin fled, leaving something greater and more anguished in its place. Kenyon must have no notion what he was offering—he must have used the word lightly, not meaning to stir long abandoned dreams, to torment with hope. And yet he had looked so vulnerable, tentative as a man addressing his new beloved. Josh wasn't sure he could bear it.

"What's the matter?" Kenyon pulled out a chair and sat close looking in Josh's face as if he actually cared about the pain.

Forcing out a curt laugh, Josh leaned his elbows on the table, unclenched his fists and tried to pull himself together; "Lovers? Did I pass out and miss that part? I must have been more overcome than I thought."

"No," said Kenyon firmly, "sarcasm aside, you've gone white as a sheet. What is it? Give me a real answer."

Gritting his teeth, Josh breathed deliberately until the complex of disbelief and desperate yearning died down enough for his voice to steady, and his stupidly romantic thoughts to come back to earth. "I'm just being an idiot— you should ignore me until the fit passes."

Neither the mockery nor the evasion worked. Peter continued to sit there, gazing at him, and as the moments lengthened, the ship swayed, reflections of rippling light slid gently to and fro across the table, and eventually the worry, the intimacy wore him down. "Even if we were to...to..."

"Become lovers."

"No!"

Josh didn't know what the word meant to Kenyon, but to him it recalled the Classics. "Lovers" was the Iliad and a young boy's dreams of glory. A book he had kept under his pillow, cherishing thoughts of war and death and timeless love. The talisman that assured him that once, once in history, even men like him had been allowed to be heroes. But that was the past, the Greeks; there was no place for such things in this modern world. If Kenyon would not be practical, then Josh must, for both their sakes.

"Even if we were to become intimate, I don't expect you to love me. We would be friends, and you would do me the favor at times, and I would do the like for you. No promises, no commitments. You will use me, sir, and I will be glad of it."

Kenyon closed his eyes in shock, opened them too soon to entirely hide a delicate distress. "Is that what you want?"

Of course not! "It's what I expect."

"But is it what you want?" Kenyon had edged closer, trying to seem reassuring, succeeding only in applying a moral pressure Josh had to brace himself not to buckle under. Despite the turmoil of his emotions, his body reacted enthusiastically to the delicious threat, and again, he was filled with disgust: *What does it matter what I want? I am no Patroclus to match your Achilles. I would show myself an utter fool trying to be worthy of you and make you a laughing stock in the process.*

"It's more than ever I hoped for."

Frustrated, Peter stood, looking down for a long heartbeat, his voice hardened by underlying anger. How he hated being trifled with! "Andrews! Is it what you *want*?"

Damn it. Damn *him!* Josh looked away, almost ready to talk about heroes and public mourning and shared tombs, choking it back because one of them had to be the realist here. But damn, damn Kenyon for making it have to be him.

Did he really want to be the one responsible for turning this fine man into a monster like himself? Did he want to take Kenyon's susceptible heart and keep it forever? Because, by God, if he once had it, he would *never* let it go. What then for Kenyon's chance at happiness? For the family he obviously desired, for the esteem and honor and status he deserved?

Everyone understood that—in famine, far from land, deprived for years from the company of women—a man might turn to his friend for ease. No one would pry too deeply into a captain relieving the loneliness of command by making a companion of his first lieutenant. But how could love be hidden? How could Kenyon hide it when he wore his feelings clear in his eyes as a summer sea? From love would come rumor. From rumor would come ruin, disgrace, and the noose.

No. No, though he was no Patroclus, to inspire a demigod to acts that would be remembered throughout history, he still had enough heroism to lie. One day, Peter would walk away from him. Peter would walk into the life that he truly wanted. And on that day he should not feel that he had ever been anything less than free.

"I can't..." and his courage failed in the light of the windows, the light of the frustration in Peter's eyes. "What if someone's listening?"

"Come with me," Kenyon lit a storm-lantern, picked something out of a cupboard and put it into his pocket. Josh wasn't sure what this mood was, but that it was daunting and desirable both at once. He followed, out of the cabin and below, down into pitch darkness, lantern light drawing lines of blued steel in Peter's black hair, illuminating the coiled hawsers of the cable tier, and the triangular room in the bow, where the barrels of rum were piled. The liquor's rich smell seeped through the wood, so strongly that the oceanic slime and drying ooze of cable became only a dash of salt among the sweet.

Kenyon gestured him to go inside. Coming close behind, Peter took the key from his pocket and locked the door after him. They were left confined together in a narrow space where to breathe was to become drunk. Heavy,

87

underwater silence pressed on the walls and the lantern light was a sphere of gold about them, an almost palpable warmth. "Private enough?"

"Yes," Josh admitted, his ribs so tight with emotion he had no room for air, let alone speech. There were only a few paces between the piled barrels and the door, and wherever he turned he ran the risk of casually brushing against his commander. Even if he stood stock still, Kenyon's presence touched him like the light. While the privacy was appreciated, these were not the best circumstances for rational thought.

Once he had hung the lantern from the hook overhead, Kenyon stood rigidly in the center of the space, hands locked behind him, shoulders square—nerving himself up. "Have you—an answer for me?" he said, formally. Then, perhaps feeling this was too intimidating, he softened slightly and smiled. "Tell me what you want, Josh. I know this sounds foolish, but I wish you joy. What can I do to make you happy?"

Josh took a deep breath that made his head swim. "May I speak plainly?" His courage was as liquid as the sea, and though he held on to it in both hands, it poured out of his grasp. How could he reply to the tenderness of such a question with the ugly words he had prepared? Yet what else could he say? "Then sir," hard to believe this had been the epitome of his ambition only yesterday, before his own expectations were so outstripped by Peter's decency. "Then, sir, I should very much like you to fuck me now and again, as an addendum to our friendship. Nothing more."

Peter took in a deep breath, unclasped his hands and bowed his head into them, shielding his face. There was a doubtful, dreadful quiet.

"I had always understood the act was—inseparable from at least a certain amount of affection," he said at last. "I should not want to be able to separate the two." Sighing, he brought the shielding hands down, to reveal eyes shaded darkly with decision and regret. "I'm not sure I can oblige you under those conditions."

The light above was mellow and comforting, the *Seahorse*'s rocking lulling, he was well fed and in the best of health, and yet Josh felt that he had never taken a worse wound. In battle, the din and the fury protected a man—dying beneath the most hideous of blows might yet be painless. But it was not so here, and it hurt.

Of course. Had he not fallen in love with Peter for this very nobility? For this strange innocent and untouched spirit, utterly alien from the sordid world Josh had learned to inhabit. Why then should he be surprised?

Counting down from twenty in poorly remembered schoolroom Latin helped him to smooth the perceptible shudder of his breathing. To make sure his eyes were dry and his face impassive, he turned away to examine a line of caulking in the deck above. He could do this with dignity, and he would—for Peter's sake and his own. "Perhaps it is for the best."

Nothing had changed after all. He had got his hopes up—vainly as it turned out—but he had lost nothing. It was sheer folly to mourn something that had never happened.

He wanted to look down, to meet Kenyon's gaze and let him see just how sincerely he meant this, but he had reached the limits of his bravery. It was, therefore, while staring at the rat-gnawed lid of the topmost barrel that he managed to say, "It is of incalculable value to me that—even knowing what I am—you were still willing to befriend me. And what I most yearn for in all the world is your society and regard. So long as I retain them, I...I am happy."

Another breath—he could no longer taste the rum on the air, but there was a meager feeling of consolation nevertheless; enough to make the second part of the statement stronger. "I have no wish to repay your goodness to me by corrupting you, by ruining your reputation, or perhaps even—God forbid—being the cause of your death."

Silence once more. A long silence and a slow change—like the loom of unseen land after months of blue water, something he could sense but could not explain. A quick glance showed Peter with the puzzled, inward look of a man chasing a revelation, hardly daring to move for fear of frightening it away. Strangely, despite the anguish and the ever present desire, a stab of amusement pricked him—how absurd this whole situation was! Was it not the final proof of man's ascendancy over nature, that his unnatural desires could be canceled out by his unnatural scruples? *Would that I were not human then.* He met Kenyon's suddenly focused gaze with a resolute, mocking smile.

But Peter's thoughts had clearly gone in quite a different direction. He closed the gap between them, and after a moment of just looking, examining Josh's face and figure with an open admiration that made heat boil into Josh's face and every part of him tingle, he raised a hand and slid it through Josh's hair. It came to rest at the nape of his neck, thumb stroking the curve of his jaw.

Trying not to shake too much, trying not to believe the best, trying not to merely melt, he arched into the touch, unable to stop himself. "Oh!"

"Josh." The dark voice was smoky with intimacy, and he could almost have died happy, just hearing his name so caressed. Instead, he looked up to meet a green gaze equally private, laced with wonder and a certain amount of rueful amusement—the traces of an understanding that had changed everything. "It occurs to me that you and I are very alike."

There was unusual warmth in Peter's face; a small, sweet smile that undermined every defense, and Josh could not help but smile back, the uneasy clamoring of his conscience temporarily forgotten.

"You're trying to protect me—and at the cost of your own happiness."

Reaching up, Kenyon took hold of the end of Josh's

cravat, pulled the bow undone and unraveled the whole, long length of it with a slow, steady pressure—a seemingly endless crisp slide of linen over Josh's skin.

Long fingers at his neck, easing open each of the buttons on his waistcoat one by one, and he could neither move nor speak for joy and lust and disbelief. If he tilted his head just slightly, he could feel Peter's breath, warm against his bared throat, he could set his mouth against the bent head and feel the cool softness of hair against his lips. He did this now, lest delay allow the chance to disappear, closed his eyes and breathed in the scent.

"So it seems to me that you already care for me, and your stipulations are intended entirely to prevent me from feeling affection for you in return. Is that right?"

Peter seemed far too coolheaded, far too in control of the situation, while Josh was fast unraveling beneath his hands. Hands that were already lifting coat and loosened waistcoat off Josh's shoulders, leaving him exposed—and so nervous that he wondered suddenly how much of his caution had been self-defense, not nobly motivated at all. Since he was being systematically bared, it seemed appropriate to surrender this, too. "Yes."

Kenyon folded the clothes and placed them carefully on the cleanest barrel. "Shall I tell you something?"

"Please."

"It's too late."

Josh needed a drink, something to steady his nerves, calm him down before he utterly committed himself to something he was persuaded was a very bad idea. What he got instead was Peter returning, having taken off his own jacket, in a shirt so worn and threadbare it was all but transparent. "W—What?"

"I already care about you, you fool. If I didn't," Peter frowned over the too-stiff little buttons of Josh's collar, undid them with practical briskness, and slid his hand under the material, watching it with curious, fascinated eyes. "If I didn't," he said, the hand closing hard, drawing Josh unresisting towards him, "would I be doing this?" He bent his head and kissed Josh's exposed throat, mouthing from shoulder to ear. And there was...teeth, and—God—tongue, and there might be a logical flaw in his argument, but Josh was too busy grabbing Peter by that worn shirt and shoving him hard into the wall to care. At the impact, Peter gave a little shudder of surprise, his breath caught and his eyes widened—Josh could feel the surrender under his hands, both of them a little taken aback by it. And delighted.

Hauling the shirt out of Peter's trousers, Josh got his hands under it. Pulling it over Peter's head, taking his hair ribbon with it, Josh threw it into a corner. Such skin! Smooth, the muscles shuddering beneath his touch. As he brushed exploratory fingers over the pale belly, Peter wriggled, snorting with laughter, and Josh remembered with a poisonous blackness that he should not be doing this.

He couldn't walk away—desire had become demand in him, insistent and barely rational—but he could at least check his wandering hands, resist the need to crowd closer, rest his forehead on the hollow of Kenyon's shoulder and try to behave less like an animal. "Your reputation? Your life!"

Peter said nothing for a while, while his agile fingers finished unlacing Josh's shirt, then he took Josh's hair and pulled until Josh had to raise his head and look at him.

"Every day on the sea, I risk life and limb and reputation for my king. May I not risk them even a little for you?"

For me? "No! Not even a little."

Kenyon caught Josh's face in both hands and leaned in to kiss—no surrender in this; it was a hard, deep kiss that left Josh broken and consumed. "It isn't your place to protect me from my own decisions, Lieutenant. It seems to have escaped your attention that *I* want this, too. I have no intention of allowing my first action on this ship to end in failure because of rank cowardice over the consequences. Now, do you want me to fuck you or not?"

And if this was what Kenyon wanted—if he wasn't merely doing it out of the goodness of his heart, to relieve a friend's pathetic need—then he should have it whatever the cost. Overcome, Josh lunged forward, wrapped his arms around Kenyon's chest, nuzzled his face into that perfect neck and hung on, while the fear that someone or something would take this away from him even now ran riot behind his tightly closed eyes. "Oh, *Peter*, yes. Please, I do."

If Kenyon was alarmed by this childish clinging, he didn't show it. Indeed, he sighed contentedly and explored Josh's back with long, leisurely, affectionate touches a world away from the impersonal groping Josh was used to. Gentle, with the habitual gentleness of a man who is only used to dealing with women. *God knows, I am behaving like one.* Josh ruefully raised his head to find Peter looking at him with a fond, slightly shy gaze.

"You'll have to show me how."

And between exaltation and the impulse to burst into tears, it was a wonder Josh retained enough wits to say, "Aye aye, sir. At once!"

Chapter Twelve

Adam Robinson paused in his examination of the repair work to watch as the HMS *Seahorse* sailed into harbor, her courses backed and then furled, her speed decreasing gently, precisely, until she dropped both anchors and stilled with as little fuss and as much elegance as a swan. Behind her, at exactly spaced lengths came the more bedraggled forms of two prizes: a snow and a thirty-two gun frigate, larger than she was herself.

Beside him, on the harbor wall, Emily stood, and her expressive eyes clouded at the sight. "Bess!" she said, on the edge of courtesy. "Stop that! You make yourself ridiculous, and me with you." For Bess was on tiptoe, waving to the incoming sailors, who festooned the rigging, grinning and whistling and waving back.

"I shouldn't resent his success, I know," said Adam slowly as Emily leaped down, clutching her skirts around her and pretending she was not hiding here in the shadow of the slipway. "But when I think that every prize makes his promotion more likely, and with it brings closer the day when he begins to take heed to your father's hints and addresses himself to you, I cannot help but wish him..."

"Not ill fortune, surely?" she said, rousing herself to tease him. He smiled with appreciation at the effort.

"Perhaps not ill. Good fortune, somewhat slowed down."

"Long enough for you to catch up."

"Indeed." He sighed. A bargain sale of the *Clara Bush*'s cargo had just about covered the cost of the repairs to her hull, but the bonus for the men of the *Nimrod* had emptied his savings from the bank, and there was nothing left with which to repair her splinted masts and torn rigging, let alone to buy a new cargo with which to begin again. He had recently had to brick up the window in the garret he lived in, to avoid window tax, and the future looked bleak.

"If I could only get her seaworthy again, there are men who would sign on for a share in the profits without wages, and I could perhaps go into debt enough to finance a trip to the slave coast. It's a business in which a man can make an easy fortune, and yet..."

"You know my feelings on that." Emily unhooked one of her earrings and looked at it, rather than at him, and though panic was a nearer companion than Adam dared admit, he still found her idealism warming.

"I do," he said, "and I share them. But Emily, you know I would marry you now if I could support you. Are you not impatient for that day?"

"I hardly know you," she said with a smile that took the sting from the words, but she reached out and fingered the fraying edge of his cuff. So light a touch, and yet he felt it in every particle of his body, like the press of sunlight. "Oh, Adam," she admitted, "if only my father were content for me to live the life I grew to adulthood in. I have no real desire to be the landed lady he wants me to be. With the money he spent on new clothes for me when we arrived, I might have opened a little shop and be now independent, free to marry who and when I chose. But would you wish to marry a shopkeeper?"

"I would wish to marry you if you were as penniless as myself," he said, gallantly, "but I could not support the idea of living off your labor. I want to lay the world at your feet, not burden you with concerns that you are too fine to bear."

Emily's mouth compressed at this, as if she had bitten into a lemon, but she said nothing, and he concluded that, like him, she was oppressed by the hopelessness of the situation. He supposed he should have withdrawn his suit at once when he discovered that she was not the nobody she claimed, but was in fact the daughter of one of the most powerful officials on the island. But by that time it had been too late; his affections were fixed.

As for hers, he noted how—despite her claim to dislike the man her father so clearly intended for her—she had now rejoined Bess on the harbor wall and was watching the doings of his ship. He took the record of repairs achieved and repairs still outstanding from the hand of his carpenter, tucked them into his partly buttoned waistcoat, and joined her.

The two prizes had dropped anchor and rocked gently in the bay. The captain's barge was lowered over the rail of the *Seahorse*, everything looking freshly painted, smart and bright beneath the blazing sky. The shrill sound of a whistle, and a small figure climbed fluidly down the side and into the boat, which rowed over to the thirty-two and collected a second figure, whose coat sparkled less brilliantly, but whose progress down the side seemed even more enthusiastic.

"I should invite him to dinner," said Emily doubtfully. "He will wonder, else, what I am doing here, and then I will come in for another interrogation as to why I will persist in being seen in your company, and why I will not think of my good name and prospects. If I go home and tell Father I came down to the harbor to invite Captain Kenyon to tea, however, he will be delighted enough not to ask more."

"Of course," Adam replied, jealousy curdling in his breast. It would be easier perhaps if his rival was ugly and stupid in addition to being successful. But the boat was close enough now that he could see Kenyon, with his patrician looks, the snowy perfection of his linen and the blaze of his gold braid. Worse, the man was deep in animated conversation with his first lieutenant, Mr. Andrews, and his normally stoic expression showed fierce pleasure, pride, and a consciousness of his own worth that Adam found intimidating. How long would any woman prefer so unheroic, unsuccessful, and unenterprising a man as himself to that?

As he thought this, Kenyon looked up and saw Emily watching. Extraordinarily, his first reaction seemed to be a flinch. The smile fell from his face. Between one breath and the next, he had presented once more the perfect mask of civility he had worn on the *Nimrod*. Adam wondered to himself was that merely the startled delicacy of a military man who has grown up among men and does not know how to behave towards women? Or was that the recoil of a guilty conscience? Of a profession for whom "out of sight, out of mind" was a daily reality?

No. No, it was unfair of him to make such an assumption simply because he wanted very much to believe this paragon had some human faults, would prove himself the worse man in the end. As a penance, he walked a little away, sitting on an abandoned coil of cable and shaking out his carpenter's report—so that Emily and Kenyon could meet in some semblance of privacy.

It did seem, as the man ran up the harbor steps to bow to Emily with a expression of shy, delighted warmth, that he had misjudged.

"I... Oh," said Kenyon, and took his hat off, looking out to sea as though an appropriate topic of conversation might be floating there. It was not. "Miss Jones."

"Captain." She dropped him a small curtsy, but cruelly left him in the lurch where conversation was concerned.

There was a long silence.

In it, Adam looked up again and caught the eye of Lt. Andrews, who stood perfectly rigid behind Kenyon. It was a shocking moment—it almost seemed to Adam that there was a physical snap as his own resentment of this meeting met that of the other man. Andrews' brown eyes seemed dark as the pit of hell, and though his face was appropriately expressionless, Adam could not hold his gaze. Adam looked away as if he had seen murder done, as if he had seen his own reflection and discovered a monster. It was deeply unsettling. Almost more so than watching the amused smile spreading on Emily's face.

"You will come to tea with my father and I? Not today, obviously, I see you have a great deal to do, but this time next week? I know he would be delighted to see you."

Kenyon's own smile answered it; a light and small expression, but on that narrow face ridiculously touching. "I should... I should be very honored, Miss Jones. My thanks."

The pit of Hell, Adam thought. Yes, that was exactly what it was like.

The pit of Hell was occupying Captain Walker's mind also. As if it wasn't enough to feel as though a carthorse had kicked him in the back, or to be so weak he could not lift a hand long enough to write a swingeing letter to the Admiralty. No, on top of all of this, the thought that they had taken his ship away from him, and they had gotten away with it, was nigh unendurable.

While he was still half lucid, in a state where reality and opium dreams mixed, Commodore Dalby had visited to tell him the *Nimrod* had sailed for England under the temporary captaincy of Dalby's cousin, and that when Walker was well enough he was to be offered instead a place administering the dockyard. At the time he had thought it a fever dream, too appalling to be real. They knew he was a fighting captain. Rodney himself had praised his fearlessness and drive; Sir George Brydges Rodney himself had recommended him for his captaincy—what the Devil's business did some paper pushing beau in London have taking it away?

But once he had recovered enough to make his voice heard, he found it was no dream. Summersgill's recommendation, Dr. Harding said, sharing the gossip that had made its way down into the officer's club. The gentleman had made a remarkable impact at the Customs Office, and Governor Bruere already thought a great deal of his judgment. Enough to invite the commodore to dinner at Government House and make the "request" to him to have Walker deprived of his ship.

At the thought, Walker was filled with such rage he almost felt well again. Summersgill? As if that cringing little civilian could be behind anything! But Summersgill's protégé? Walker was not blind to the affection in which Summersgill held Kenyon. Talking and plotting together all the way from Portsmouth! Kenyon had been trouble from the start, with his dramatics and his "more perfect than thou" attitude. It was surely no coincidence that the threat of mutiny had never been more prevalent than on this last voyage with that poisonous young man as first lieutenant.

Now Kenyon had a ship, and his string of prizes was the talk of the hospital. He and Andrews, that sick little pervert, were getting rich, while Walker himself lay bereft and disgraced with nothing but a small sugar plantation and a few hundred slaves, and a job at the *dockyard*, for pity's sake, like an invalid or a *tradesman.* It could not be borne.

Andrews! He had had that abomination's neck practically in the noose. He hadn't forgotten the look of terror on the boy's face at Henderson's hanging. It was one of the few pleasant things he had to meditate on in this place. And now the midshipman had become a first lieutenant, raking in prize money and glory, with the world entirely ignorant of his disgusting little secret.

Why had Kenyon not discovered it yet? Was he too blind, as some over-genteel country bumpkins were, to recognize what he saw? Was he corrupt enough to overlook

99

it, as were some of the effete men of the town?

Or was he... Walker took in a long breath of realization, gasped at the pain, then coughed and coughed, eyes streaming and the dull ache in his back woken up into red hot agony once more. Damn this injury! Damn this place of sickness where he felt as effectively imprisoned as he might in a French cell. When the fit wore off, he lay down, trembling, and finished the thought with a smile.

Or was he implicated? Kenyon didn't look like a filthy bugger, but then so few of them did. But if they were at it together, then a few encouraging words and coins offered to the disaffected members of the *Seahorse*'s crew should have them both.

Walker drifted off to sleep to visions of the two of them, tied back to back, one noose around both throats, slowly throttling together in the busy naval bustle of Ordnance Island, on the gallows, looking out on a fleet glad to be cleansed of them. Such a satisfying dream! He woke smiling.

Chapter Thirteen

"That was encouragement." Peter smiled at his own reflection in the small mirror he had propped against his sea chest in the corner of their attic room, while Josh—still painfully jealous—pretended not to have heard him.

The landlady came grumbling up the stairs with a couple of jugs of warm water and poured one into the basin before Peter, then smiled a fox's smile. "Nice to have you back, gents. I did hear you was come into a small fortune on account of that thirty-two was stuffed with guns for the rebels. Wish you joy if that's so, and have you thought of taking the larger room downstairs?"

"Thank you, Mrs. Hodges," said Josh, once he realized that Peter was too taken up in his own thoughts to reply. "I'm sure Captain Kenyon will consider it, when he has had time to wash the salt off and isn't so perished with hunger."

"Ah, as to food," she said, pretending not to look as Peter took off his wig and placed it on the stand, "how it stands as far as to food is this..."

Josh wasn't in the mood to listen to another improbable litany of bad luck that would end with them having no dinner. "We will dine at the Cat and Fiddle," he interrupted, with the firm voice he had cultivated to command the prize crew on the thirty-two "and speak to you about accommodations afterwards." *Hopefully to say we are moving out.* Pointedly, he held the door open.

When she had gone, he crossed over to his side of the room, took off his own wig and put it in its box. Folding his coat over his sea chest, he unbuckled his breeches at the knees, and sat down on his mattress, hugging himself for comfort.

"Meeting me at the harbor," Peter insisted in a dreamy, contemplative voice. "It was encouragement."

Peter was, Josh thought, trying to concentrate on the way the reinforced stitching around his knees pressed into his cheek, not a cruel man. He was not doing this in order to hurt Josh, whatever it might feel like. No, Peter was not cruel, but he was, at times, horribly oblivious, and it could amount to much the same thing.

Peter looked worried now at the lack of response. Josh could feel the gaze on his bent head like two searching points of light. He could tell that some of his own misery had finally penetrated that noble but thick head from the almost silent way Peter unfolded himself to standing, took the two steps that separated his domain from Josh's, and knelt, hand on the mattress next to Josh's stockinged foot, his knee next to it, bowing the bed and tilting Josh towards him.

"What is it?" said Peter, genuinely at a loss.

And after all, Josh thought, could Peter really be blamed for misunderstanding, when Josh had deliberately tried to mislead him? It was irrational to hope that somehow Peter would read in the silences all the words Josh refused to speak; *I don't want you to love her; I want you to love* me. *I don't want you to leave me. Stay with me forever!*

Stupid words that could never be said. It was wrong of him to even cherish them in his heart, five hundred times worse to say them. He should rejoice that Peter at least could leave this sin behind, go forward into a welcome respectability, with a wife to love him and children to connect him to the future. He did not have the right to want to take all that away, imprison Peter forever in a world of lies and shame. He should be a better man than that.

"It's nothing, sir," Josh said at last, when he had successfully fought down the clawing protestations of his own selfishness. "I'm just a little out of sorts."

He thought of Mr. Robinson, with whom he had shared a brief but intense moment of jealousy, and wondered whether he should pour a more rational restraint on the rejoicing. Should he say, "But do not get your hopes up, I think she has another admirer, and perhaps a more favored one?" For Kenyon had the blindness of privilege. Obstacles removed themselves from his path, and he had not yet learned how to see them.

Josh did not want to be the man who taught him. If Josh had his way, he would be the force that leveled Peter's path ahead of him and removed the stones, so that he did not even bruise his feet on his journey to greatness. But Josh wondered if that too was selfish. He wondered, often, whether it might be better for Peter, and the world, if Joshua Andrews was removed from it. But always when the knife was in his hand, he would pause and think of the torments of Hell, and fear held him back. Better to sit here, with the attic windows open and the whitewashed garret filled with light, trying to enjoy Peter's closeness without hoping to possess it, than to cut it all short for something worse.

"What can I do," Peter's long-fingered hand closed on his ankle, then slid gently, teasingly up his calf, rolling the silk down and repeating the operation on skin, "to make you feel better?"

At the touch, bitter lust came boiling up from within him. Josh gulped a great breath against the tightness in his chest, raised his head and rested it against the wall, closed his eyes so that Peter would not see the anguish—for even he was not *that* blind—and reached out. His fingers tangled in newly brushed hair, pointed with dampness, and he pulled the hair ribbon out so that black silk strands would sweep forward and enclose Peter's face.

Peter gave a soft, small chuckle and leaned in, his lips gentle on Josh's forehead and his closed eyes, less gentle, less chaste as they worked their way down the angle of his jaw and to his neck. Josh's entire soul seemed to be concentrated in the patch of skin beneath Peter's mouth. Everything else hurt. It hurt to think, his chest felt as though the veins were severed and every beat of his heart was filling it with blood, and he whimpered, undoing Peter's cravat and shirt buttons with silent desperation, as if Peter's skin could heal him.

Peter laughed again, and drew away. Josh opened his eyes to find the man walking over to the door, locking it against prying visitors. Josh filled his eyes with the sight of that strong, slender back, the dark hair falling to a point between his shoulder blades, the light of the windows sifting through the finely woven shirt, hinting at the plains of Peter's chest. Josh breathed in again, his own skin waking up, feeling the press of his clothes like a tantalizing caress that did nothing but make him itch for more. His fingers tangled in his neck-cloth, pulling the bow into a knot, and he yanked it savagely before abandoning it and tearing his shirt off without it, the cloth still knotted about his neck.

"You're always so...eager," said Peter, with a smile, as though this was praise. It seemed it was. "I love that." He took hold of the neck-cloth and pulled Josh's face to his own, and Josh, who wanted the kiss to take away the feeling that he was bleeding to death, drowned in it gladly.

"Shirt off," Josh demanded, pulling at it impatiently while Peter wriggled his wrists out from the lace cuffs. When it was thrown into the center of the room, he could finally lock his arms around Peter's back and pull the man down on top of him, wanting to be crushed by the weight. Every inch of skin that touched Peter felt alive, every part that did not was a howling wilderness, and he trembled between them feeling that he would break apart with the need and the anguish and the joy of it.

Catching his fever, Peter knelt up to unbutton both pairs of breeches, shove them down, before lying down again, bare prick hard against Josh's. Josh cried out, some part of his purgatory escaping his control in a pleading little whine of need, and he hated himself for this, he hated... He thrust up against Peter, witless and instinctive, his eyes closing from the wave of pleasure, the bliss and horror of it. Sensing Josh's mood, Peter bowed his head and bit Josh's shoulder, and the spike of pain mixed with the stroking, building pulse of pleasure, where they slid together, making it feel honest, permitted, *real*.

Wordlessly, Josh spread his legs, asking for more, the knowledge that this might be the last time winning out effortlessly over the reluctance to beg, and when Peter tried to reach for oil, Josh panicked and would not let him, winding himself around the man, holding on as hard as he could, until Peter, moved by some instinct more aware than his reason muttered "Shh, I'm not going anywhere," and slicked himself with spit instead.

It was a brutal coupling. Looking for something to hold onto, Peter's hands found the neck-cloth, twisted it until Josh could hardly breathe. The burn and hot piercing pain of penetration made him want to scream with pleasure and gasp and writhe and demand more, and the thought that Peter was choking him, the punishment so infinitely deserved, so lovingly bestowed, made tears leak from the edges of his eyes. Josh wrenched at Peter's hair and bit his mouth and wriggled backwards, impaling himself on Peter's strength. He came like dying, in a rush of surrender that, just for one moment, overwhelmed the self-disgust and let him feel clean.

"You're a sick little bastard," said Peter, afterwards, as they lay together in the sunshine, lazily kissing. His tone of voice said "I love you", but Josh was more inclined to believe his words.

"I know."

"Oh, now," Peter raised himself on an elbow and looked down, his eyes full of concern, his hair ink dark, spilling over his shoulder, "I meant it affectionately."

Josh had to laugh at that. How could the man possibly remain so terrifyingly innocent, so pure, after what they had just done? He shifted on the mattress, fished out from beneath him a pulled off button and felt the moment of peace begin to unravel. "So," he whispered, "you have the money to buy a house now. Will we not be sharing any more?"

"Is that what this was about?" Peter looked enlightened. He smoothed the tangled curls from Josh's forehead with a tender hand, leaned down and kissed where he had bitten. "I think that would be a little precipitate, don't you? No, it's true I was thinking of moving away from Mrs. Hodges curiosity and her non-existent catering, but I am hoping that, whereever I go, you will come with me."

Chapter Fourteen

Next week saw Adam and Emily meet in the marketplace in King's Square. She had a jaunty little hat of lace on top of her carefully dressed blond hair, and it threw a pattern of shadowed flowers onto her face. There was one right in the center of her full lower lip in particular that seemed to taunt him. His eyes refused to settle elsewhere, and if he managed to wrench them away, they would stray to the gauzy fichu that protected her milk white breasts from the sun. And that lead to thoughts more appropriate for private darkness than for conversation with a delicate young lady. He could not help feeling that he must shock and unsettle her.

She concealed it well, however, if it was so, set her parasol on her shoulder and strolled down the stalls of produce with a radiant smile, Bess following behind with a basket and a disapproving look.

"May I talk to you alone, Miss Jones?" he asked, turning over the rabbit's foot in his pocket which had so far brought him such singular bad luck, but which was all he had to turn to in this moment of decision.

Her smile edged with curiosity, she said "Bess, go down and buy me a shilling's worth of those beautiful oranges, will you? Oh, and tell One-Eyed Sam I'll be down in a moment to pay for the lobsters."

Such a capable young woman. He had admired her bravery on board ship, after the battle, but he admired too how easily she had adapted to this strange country, and her calm and businesslike dealings with creditors, suitors and her foster mother—still prostrated by the heat and unable to rise from her bed. Emily was not a romantic girl, who might be swept away by emotion, and though he had the highest opinion of her because of that, this was a moment when he felt he might prefer it were so.

Walking past the pillory without paying any attention to the poor wretch who stood there, covered in refuse and bruises, he paused in front of the town hall and looked up as if to admire the architecture. When she came to his side, still with shadow roses on her lips, his nerve almost failed. What he meant to suggest was foolish in the extreme, and might well be interpreted as immoral, but at present he could see no other way forward.

"Miss Jones," he said, solemnly, looking from the dazzling white walls to her more dazzling face. "Will you marry me?"

A glow began in her blue eyes that made them rival the tropical sky for intensity, and she leaned forward, placing her hand on his wrist. Not on the cuff, but on the skin. There was a little shock of connection and he felt enlarged, powerful, exhilarated—ready to be swept away by joy. But what she said was, "Something has changed? That's wonderful! What has happened to make you ready to dare this step?"

Her faith was like a slap in the face, and he thought resentfully that he had not said that. He had asked a simple question to which he might have preferred a simple answer. But that was unfair. Despair was driving him to be unfair, these days; his temper was short and his manners snappish.

"Nothing has changed, alas," he said. *But that you invited Kenyon into your house, and today he will attempt to storm your heart as he stormed through that privateer at sea, with your father holding all the doors open for him.* "But that I can't stand the waiting any more. The truth is

that I don't ever see things changing for the better and..."
And I want to make sure of you before someone else does.

"And you are ready to use my dowry to open a shop?" Her look of delight had clouded but was still uncomfortably hopeful.

He was insulted by the suggestion. "I am not a fortune hunter, Miss Jones. I would not accept a penny of your money were I starving in the street."

It was hard to believe that a face as beautiful as hers— so round and merry, soft as swan's down—could become suddenly so shrewish and so harsh. "What then?" she said. "Shall we live on, air? I wonder you expect my father to fall in with such a suggestion. It would take much working upon him to persuade him to see me settled with a tradesman, though I assured him day and night it was what I knew and would prefer. But what? To marry and expect him to support us both? I do not see how that would be any more admirable."

The justice of this rebuke struck Adam to the heart, and it was too hard to bear, receiving disappointment at her hands as well as from the rest of the world. Rather than apologize, he stood up straighter, locked his hands behind his back and said, "I am not proposing to ask your father for either upkeep or permission. I am suggesting that we present him with a fait accompli. Come away with me into the hills, there is a little chapel there at which the priest will marry us without banns or witnesses. It could be done tomorrow, and no one the wiser."

Emily took a step backwards and her mouth fell open into an "o" of disbelief, then she shut it with a snap and tossed her highly coiffed head. "Am I to understand you are suggesting we *elope*, Mr. Robinson? Am I to understand that you are suggesting I deceive my father not merely now, but for an untold number of years afterwards?"

Looking at her then, he began to understand why Victory was always depicted as a woman. She was not large, and there were times, previously, when she had put him in mind of a kitten, soft and playful, affectionate. But now there was a light of martial glory about her. Perhaps it was merely her eloquence that made him feel small, tongue-tied and guilty as a boy standing before his mother, convicted of stealing cake from the larder. She was clad in light white muslin, but it might as well have been armor, and her tongue was all the sword she needed.

"No," she said, scornfully, "I know what it is. You do not trust me."

Struck to the heart by this, Adam opened his mouth to protest that of course he trusted her, but the words eluded him as she went on.

"You do not trust me to wait for you until your fortunes are repaired. What advantage otherwise is there in a marriage we conceal from all, but to take away from me my power of choice? I thought better of you, Mr. Robinson. I thought you understood that my regard for you is freely and willingly given but *cannot be compelled*."

It was hard to listen to this when she should know that he loved her. Had he not just proposed? What more proof of his regard did she need? What more did she expect from him? And yet as she broke off and turned partly away to conceal the gulping down of tears, another part of him was furious at himself for hurting her, for making her look like this. He stepped forward and reached out to take her hand, but she wrenched it away and turned fully, leaving him to converse with the nape of her neck, and even that seemed to radiate affront, as if to tell him that he was not wanted here any more.

"You are just as bad as all the rest of them," she hissed. "If I am to be treated as a possession no matter what I do, I do not know why I should not sell myself to the highest bidder. If you will not let me earn my own bread and have my own choice, how are you different from my father and Kenyon?"

With her back turned, she missed the flush of anger that Adam could feel scald into his face, driving out thoughts of how hurt she must be to say these things, replacing them only with thoughts of how little she must care for him to want to wound him so.

"If I must be a prize, why should I not marry Kenyon? He would at least give me a carriage and servants and a comfortable life and be gone to sea three months out of every four, so I might have my freedom in his absence."

"Oh, is that your answer indeed?" Adam resisted the urge to throw his hat onto the ground and trample on it by instead pulling on his cuff until the lace separated beneath his fingers. He had to tear something, and the strip of linen made a gratifying struggle before ripping.

"As you wish! Then I offer you joy of my own absence, since that is the freedom you seem to crave. By all means marry where you see fit. I am only sorry that you are so repulsed by my own offer as to hurl yourself into the arms of a man you professed to dislike. But perhaps—as with your affection for me—your dislike for him will prove strictly temporary. I hope your future life is to your satisfaction, Miss Jones. Good day."

She did not turn back to watch him walk away, and he, striding out with the ferocious energy of anger, had reached the entrance to Water Street before he realized that she was not going to follow. Pausing there, his better nature urged him to go back, to speak gently to her and have her smile at him again. But pride forbade him. He had nothing left but his pride, neither ship nor stores nor—now—hope, and he refused to allow any of it to make him crawl.

Chapter Fifteen

The light of the hot tropic sun flooded through the windows of the orangery and glinted from the rope of pearls which Emily had wound into her corn gold hair. Peter uncrossed his ankles and looked for inspiration at the tawny surface of his tea, trying to think of something to say. Miss Jones was in wonderful looks today, with a very attractive blush glowing on her cheeks, but she seemed less outspoken than he had known her to be before. He could not conclude in his mind whether this was a good sign or a bad.

"So tell me again about your latest acquisitions," said Summersgill, rising to help himself from the plate of sugared fruit which sat on the table between them. Summersgill had a more rounded look to him now. It seemed that the punishing climate suited him. "I understand it was the thirty-two which was smuggling arms?"

Peter blessed him for his tact. As he had already been through the exact cargo manifest and the potential contacts at either end of the trade route with Summersgill in his professional capacity, this could only be a rescue from the way his mind went blank when expected to be witty and entertaining.

"The *Macedonian*, yes," Peter said. "I had a tip off from one of the men at the docks—I took his brother on recently as cook, and in gratitude, he suggested the ship should be watched. We intercepted it a little over fifty miles off shore from Boston, and when we made our signal, rather than prepare for inspection, they bolted for shore.

"But the *Seahorse*, as you know, is a fine ship for sailing close hauled, and had fully two points on her. We came up close into the wind, caught her within three miles and gave her a raking broadside, stern to stem. She surrendered at once, and once we got on board it was clear why—powder barrels five deep on every deck. The wonder of it was that she hadn't gone sky high with our first shots."

The warm, bright room became, in his mind, the cool brilliance of his quarterdeck. He could almost feel the life of the ship beneath him, hear the cheers, see again the berserker joy on Josh's face as he returned from the boarding party with a bruise on his face—where the *Macedonian's* captain had tried fighting back with a crowbar—and a blaze of fierce beauty in his brown eyes.

Thinking of Josh, Peter smiled to himself, proud that the young midshipman had proved not only an exemplary first lieutenant, but shown himself, on this trip, more than capable of captaining a ship of his own.

Though that thought had its own bitterness. If the *Macedonian* was brought into the service, he knew he should recommend Josh for her commander. But at the thought, Peter suddenly understood why his lover had been so needy recently. Time had reached the point where it would be natural for them to part; to purchase houses of their own, to captain ships of their own, to speak to one another only on those rare occasions when they were both on shore together.

He didn't know why this came as a shock. Nor why it should suddenly strike him now, here of all places. It had always been meant as a strictly temporary arrangement, of course. But he had somehow also managed to avoid the thought of it ever ending, to avoid the thought that he might one day have to choose to give Josh up in order to take a wife and remain faithful to her.

For he couldn't have both. Could he?

A tap on his knee, and he looked up, startled to find Summersgill's eyes trained on him in some concern and Emily watching him with a new born curiosity.

"Are you well?" Summersgill asked gently.

"I'm sorry." Peter shook his head and tried out one of his more polite smiles. He looked at Summersgill's kindly face, and then the subdued beauty of his daughter. Emily's expression was quite composed, but her fingers were pulling the petals from one of the table dressings, scattering them on the tablecloth like huge drops of blood. *No*, he thought, looking at her and seeing for the first time some sort of discomfort, nobly borne, he could not have both. That would be unfair to both, and besides, damaging to his own honor.

Even so, he didn't want to think about it yet. There were some weeks...months...perhaps even years yet before the decision would become impossible to put off any longer, and with that comforting thought, he roused himself to be civil and make an effort.

"Do forgive me; I must be excessively dull today, unable to talk about anything but battles. Tell me, Miss Jones, did you finish reading *Julia de Roubigne*? I hoped its abolitionist sentiments would appeal, even if Mackenzie's language is a little...affected."

Emily looked up with surprise and gave him a smile that, by its sweetness, set into contrast the forced gestures she had used towards him previously. It almost made him wonder if, perhaps, she had not liked him before, which was a sobering sentiment. But if that was so, he consoled himself, she did seem to be coming around. The pleasure of putting delight on Summersgill's face, and of raising Emily's subdued spirits to something more like their usual pitch, made him forget Josh once more and exercise his mind upon literature for the rest of the visit.

He left with a promise to return and a feeling of

satisfaction that everything was going very much to plan.

"Reverend Jenson," Captain Walker welcomed his guest to dinner and fed him on turtle soup, beef and lamb, roast and stewed and flavored with spices, a brace of birds he had shot with his own gun, plum duff, figgy dowdy, jellies of lime and oranges, and a resplendent pineapple, accompanied by tea and coffee, madeira, claret, Nantes and Aguardiente. They were alone for the meal—except, of course, for the phalanx of servants—and he did not scruple to talk business over the meat.

"I hope you will not mind if I address a delicate topic? It is a scandal, sir, how our reluctance to even think about this sin is our greatest hurdle to dealing with it, but I know of you as a man of principle. I read eagerly in the *Times* of your prosecution of that villainous fellow Franklin."

"Oh," Reverend Jenson put down his knife and fork and nodded with an air of understanding, "now I see why you did not extend your invitation to my wife. Yes, it is a topic from which the ladies should be protected with the greatest care. That they should not know it exists at all has always been my ideal, but I take your point. Our reticence should not become a shield behind which these disgusting practices can shelter.

"I remember," he continued, his face glowing with pride, "that in my father's day, the Society for the Reformation of Manners used to prosecute hundreds of the creatures by the month, but ever since the societies were disbanded—perhaps, as you say, through an excess of delicacy, or as I saw it, the sheer fatigue of wading through such dirt for so long—they have thought themselves safe."

"Indeed." at the slight tilt of Walker's head, a servant rushed up to replenish the food on his plate. He kept them well trained or not at all. "Did you know," he said, slicing his meat into small pieces and chewing one before dabbing

115

his mouth with a fine linen napkin and continuing, "there is even a molly house on Silk Alley in St. George's itself."

"No! Not in our town, surely. So far from the depravity of London?"

"God's truth." Walker raised his hand as if swearing an oath, and found himself feeling unusually content—oh, certainly the docklands job was an insult, and there were many feuds on his hands which he had not yet prosecuted to their utmost, but it was pleasant to sit and eat a good dinner with a man who was not always criticizing, either by words or looks. One who was appropriately conscious of the condescension paid him by being enlisted in this enterprise at all. "I have seen the place myself and had one of my tars feign to be a bugger himself and infiltrate the place. I know of what I speak."

"But this is terrible!" Jenson pushed the good food in front of him about with his fork and—perhaps in horror— did not eat. Walker's feeling of unusual beneficence wore off at the sight; he did dislike a stingy, stringy little falsely abstemious man. It was an affront against hospitality to treat his dinner with such disregard.

"No wonder we are troubled with rebellion in our Colonies," Jenson went on. "If what you say is true—and, my dear sir, believe me, I have no doubt of it—we are being justly punished by God for our depravities. If we put them behind us, grubbed their dark roots from our land, so to speak, what might that not do to turn the tide of affairs in the Americas? We would surely bring them to a proper submission once more, once God approved the righteousness of our spirits."

"We are of one mind," Captain Walker said, raising his glass with only a little effort. Reverend Jenson's heart was in the right place, whatever might be said for his stomach, and parsons, of course, could not be expected to behave like real men. "I suggest we begin by rousing up popular opinion against it; the example of Sodom and Gomorrah,

116

the unquenched spreading of the pox, the danger to our innocent sons. And then we may prove that the great days of the societies are not over by going after these abominations with extreme zeal, confident that a population educated in the dangers they pose will not interfere with ill-judged pity."

"My text today is taken from Genesis, chapter nineteen, verses one to twenty-nine."

Peter's attention was drawn back from the ceiling by the tension in Josh's arm, pressed against his in the overcrowded pews set aside for the gentlemen of the navy. He looked down and saw Reverend Jenson dwarfed by the giant eagle of the lectern, looking like a rather withered choirboy beneath the crimson glory of his chasuble. Seeing nothing to disturb him there, he glanced at Andrews, whose back had straightened until it rivaled the oak of the pews, and whose face was perfectly emotionless in a way that Peter had learned to associate with fear.

Bending his head, as if in prayer, he whispered, "What is it?" and Josh gave him such a look—such a look of indignant terror, as if to say, "Shut up! Shut up, don't draw attention!" that he had to concentrate on the sermon in an attempt to escape its unsettling effects.

But the sermon did not help. "Before they had gone to bed, all the men from every part of the city of Sodom, both young and old, surrounded the house. They called to Lot, 'Where are the men who came to you tonight? Bring them out to us so that we can have sex with them.'"

It was like the wind of a cannon ball—the shot passed by and left him physically unscathed, but within, all his vitals were thrown into disorder and he gasped for breath. Instantly, he felt as though there was a string of signal flags above him pointing him out to the crowd as a guilty man. A man as bad as those who so long ago tried to rape God's angels, a man whose vice was vile enough to call down brimstone and sulfur from heaven, to induce a merciful God to obliterate him and his city together.

"...we are going to destroy this place. The outcry to the Lord against its people is so great that he has sent us to destroy it."

Oh, he knew the story well enough. He had merely avoided connecting it to himself, found something else to think about, falsely reasoned that making Joshua happy was better than ruining the lives or reputations of any young women.

"What can we learn from these verses?" said Jenson's polite, Anglican voice over Peter's suddenly bowed head. "Firstly, I think it is clear enough that God detests this sin above all others. For no other sin has he utterly destroyed a people, leaving even the land on which their city was built as a desolation, salting the ground so that nothing should grow there ever again."

Peter's legs were stretched out beneath the pew in front, thigh to thigh with Josh's, their calves touching. Instinctively, he moved until there was an inch of empty space between them and saw Josh's head bow out of the corner of his eye. Around him, other men were doing the same, tucking their coat tails more firmly in, looking uncomfortable, but he felt still that the very air between himself and Josh was charged with visible guilt.

"Secondly, we can learn to fear the presence of such men in our midst. I have reliably been told that there is a den of this vice on Silk Alley in our very own town. Now you may say to yourself that is very far from being all the men of St. George's, both young and old. Will not God—looking at our city—be able to find at least ten righteous men, and thus spare us?

"Folly, I say, for how can the toleration of this vice count as righteousness? And in this sin, every one of us is complicit. While there remains such an establishment permitted in our city, there is not an innocent man in it, and that is quite apart from the patrons of such a sink. It is of no avail to say, 'Oh, this is a problem of others, none of my acquaintance would sink so low', for does not the Bible tell us that both young and old, all the men of Sodom were implicated. It spreads, my children, like the yellow fever, until it consumes all. Indeed, it is a very sickness of the soul, and as we fumigate our hospitals with sulfur, so God purges this disease from the land."

Disease, thought Peter, wishing he could escape, feeling exposed and humiliated as he had felt when lashed to the grating. No, this was worse, for there he had had the internal certainty that he was wronged, that he was a victim of sin, not the perpetrator of it. It could be a disease. He could have caught it from Allenby in his youth, been re-infected by Andrews; one in a long line of victims until he became a carrier himself.

"With this certainty, we may reexamine our current peril," Jenson was saying, still with the clear voice and clear conscience of a man who has never even felt tempted to this sin, who congratulates himself on his feelings of disgust. "Many have asked how we could lose the Americas. Why the colonists would wish to separate themselves from their own homelands and their families left behind in Britain. Many of you, I know, have asked yourself whether we were safe here on this little island, with so small a naval force protecting us, or whether we will suffer invasion and dispossession and death.

"Well, I say to you that our safety does not depend on navies, not even on distant kings, but on the direct protection of God. How long can we go on angering him and expect to remain secure?"

There were stern and frightened faces about him now, some serious looks and nodding, and he felt each one as an accusation. More than that, he became aware of the darkness above him in the vault of the roof, the heavy stones, the bells above, and everywhere he looked he seemed to find condemnation, as though the very stones cried out against him.

The service passed in a blur of hot self-awareness. When it ended, and he found himself filing out, expected to shake the vicar's hand, he felt the light should expose him and the touch detect his trembling.

"How refreshing it is," said Josh before him, taking the man's hand with a bravery that humbled Peter, "to hear a man condemn a sin in which he has no part. With what joy one can join in its persecution, knowing that one has no share in it. No fellow-feeling for the sinner."

Reverend Jenson clearly did not hear the rebuke in this remark. He nodded and smiled, and seeing him so fooled, Peter was able to shake his hand with some confidence, but it was still an escape when he turned the corner into Duke of Clarence Street and could no longer feel the presence of the church behind him.

He fell into step with Josh, and they walked together down towards Ordnance Island and along the causeway, sea on either side, the *Macedonian* tied up against the quay, and the *Seahorse* out in the bay, her racing lines silhouetted against water as burningly bright as a sheet of mercury. All the time, he felt a stranger in his own body, a prisoner in his own mind, unable to know what to do. He had been in a kind of Eden before the serpent, somehow unaware on a conscious level of what he was doing. But now he had eaten of the tree of the knowledge of good and evil and knew that he should be ashamed.

Peter had always been a good boy; dutiful, responsible, truthful, willing to work hard for himself and for others, and he had never had a great deal of experience of guilt. It came upon him now as a calamity.

"We should talk," he said, finally breaking the silence that had lain between them for the last two miles.

"I know what you're going to say," said Josh with some

of that same bitter, black humor he had used on Jenson. He raised his head and smiled the smile of a condemned man. "The time had come anyway. This thing between us had run its course—it was time to move on, regardless. Was it going to be 'we can still be friends?' or 'perhaps we'd better make it a clean break'?"

The dreadful, cold mockery of this added another level of pain and shame to the whirlpool in Peter's breast. "Josh!" he cried, feeling shocked and a little betrayed—as it was Josh himself who had given him the impression he expected nothing from him beyond the occasional recreational fuck.

"I'm sorry," said Josh and his voice shook suddenly, making repentance and pity stab through Peter's confused heart. "You're right. I knew this was coming, and I'm glad." He turned his back, but not before Peter had seen the twist of his brows, the compression of his fine oval mouth that gave the lie to his "gladness".

"I'm sorry, too," said Peter, hardly knowing what he said in his desire to make everything right at once. "I shouldn't have...I shouldn't have begun something with you had I known it would cause you such pain to end it. I shouldn't have been so inconstant. Forgive me?"

Josh walked away, back to the steps that ran down to the beach. The white sand was strewn with rubbish, and he stopped, his head turned towards a straggle of nets, his back to Peter. But Josh's back was eloquent, and its cowed tension told Peter that he would have done better not to speak at all.

"Are you telling me you regret there was ever anything between us?" Josh asked.

"If it provoked you to disappointment. If it made you feel as I feel now, then, yes. I would not have given you such pain had I not thoughtlessly used you to satisfy my own curiosity, my wanton need."

Josh laughed—a cynical sound—but did not turn round. Even the animation of anger was gone when he next spoke, his voice weary and dull. "I could only wish you were sorry for finishing with me, rather than for ever starting."

Damn him, why did he always have to take everything wrongly? A small part of Peter considered the fact that it might not the best time for apologies—while he was guilt-stricken and overemotional, terrified of God, man and himself. Sighing, he rubbed the bridge of his nose, walked close enough to see Josh's mobile face gone shuttered and unreadable.

"I don't think you understand, sir," said Josh in a quiet, charged voice. "The world doesn't allow men like me to hope for constancy. I never expected it. You're going to marry. I did expect that. And I'll be glad to see you happy."

He walked down onto the sand, Peter following, torn between the certainty that he must go through with this, and the certainty that if he let Josh go—if he lost Josh, he could not survive it.

"I don't have any *claim* on you, Peter. I never asked for your *fidelity*. I only want..." Josh's breath hitched, betraying some of the misery concealed behind that blank expression. The dark eyes glittered for a moment, then shut, concealing tears. "I want whatever's left over. I'll take anything. Friendship, if that's all your conscience will allow. But I don't...I don't want you to tell me you regret ever having known me at all."

"It's not..." Touching his arm, Peter chased after the right words, frustrated with his own stupidity. "Not what I meant. Oh, damn it...you know I'm no good at this stuff. Give me an enemy in my sights and a blue water chase, and I'll know what to do, but I... Oh, I am hopeless when it comes to love."

Caught in the act of ducking into the shadow of the pier, Josh's step faltered, his mouth and eyes rounded in wonderment, and he stood dumbstruck. It was such a rare occurrence, that even in his half-coherent state, Peter knew he must have said something extraordinary. He worked out what it was just at the point when Josh's expression became a rather dazzled smile.

"Love?" Josh whispered, while his spirit seemed to have caught the fire of the sun, gone golden and remote.

"I suppose it is...was...*is*," said Peter, wearily marveling at the way joy made Josh's rather nondescript face look bright and fierce, lending him an inner radiance, a sort of beauty. Such a little thing—surely he must have said it before? And perhaps it would have been better left unsaid at that, for it solved nothing. "But a forbidden love. It was not wrong to love you, but we did wrong to express it as we did. If I am married, and we are in separate ships, I will still love you, for I have never had a worthier friend."

It was cool in the shadow of the pier, and the wet pylons around them smelled sharply of oak and salt, and there boiled up from Peter's imagination the picture of him taking Josh's face between his hands and kissing him soundly, lying him down on the cool, damp sand and showing him with all the force in his body exactly what love was.

The picture left as swiftly as it had come, leaving him shaking, hard, and determined that if either of them were to escape the noose, separate ships were a vital necessity. "But perhaps you were right, earlier, and we should find ourselves lodgings apart—to make it easier to set this sin aside, lest we prove each other's ruin."

Chapter Sixteen

"There's someone alive in there!"

Josh could hear it, too, as sparks poured into the air, smoke and flame turning the whole night into a yellow amber confusion that smelled of unbreathable reek and burning flesh. Above the roaring of flame a man's voice shrieked, inhuman, desperate, and Josh broke through the line of prostitutes and their customers, passing pitchers and chamber pots of water from hand to hand from the well to the fire. He tore off his cravat, dumped it in a basin of water and, wrapping it round his face, he ran up the steps to number four Silk Alley and into its spacious reception hall.

Velvet curtains hung in rags of black ash against walls that smoldered beneath the plaster. The room was so full of smoke he could see the stairs only because they were burning, pulling away from the walls, threatening to collapse on the heads of the few men who had made it this far. At the top of the impassable staircase, the screaming grew raw, frantic and agonized. Josh tried to force himself onto the inferno that was the stairs, closed his eyes, ran for it, and was pulled back by powerful hands.

"Nothing we can do, cully." The man who had his right arm was a carpenter, and bizarrely, a man he had known in London. A silent look of recognition and complicity passed between them. "I hope the fucking bastards are proud of themselves, that's all I can say. C'mon before it gets us, too."

The man on his left looked up, just as the bestial, bubbling scream was mercifully cut off, and Josh was amazed to see that it was Adam Robinson, soot streaks through his blond hair and his eyes red with smoke.

Outside it felt cold. They joined the lines of folk laboring to quench the fire before it spread to the neighboring houses, and when the roof finally fell and the bonfire began to eat itself from within, Josh—moved by the impulse of shared danger—touched Robinson's arm and said, "Let's find some breakfast."

Robinson looked up at where the sun's early rays were turning the charred skeleton of building from the overpowering monster of the night into a sad and sordid wreck. "I..." he said and coughed the racking early morning cough of a heavy smoker. Around them a hundred other people were doing the same. "I am not sure I..."

It was something of a comfort to Josh to find a man who seemed to be suffering even more than he himself was. Pleasant though it might have been to find all his cares resolved and his heartache mended, it was a good second place to feel that he might be of assistance to someone else. His sharp eye caught the frayed cuffs of Robinson's suit and the gauntness of his face, and he added quickly, "You must allow me to buy you breakfast, both for saving my life in there and in celebration of my good news."

The exaggeration made the man laugh, his anxious look becoming a smile of great charm. "I hardly saved your life, Lieutenant."

"I was fully determined to climb those stairs," said Josh, shivering at the memory. "You brought me to a consciousness of how foolish it would be. I have no doubt, that if you had not been there, I would have been consumed." *Partly,* b*ecause I would not have cared enough to live.* "Besides, sir, you mistake my rank. It is captain, now."

"No!" Robinson's surprise and unfeigned pleasure brought a smile to Josh's face, but he was conscious that it was not wise for either of them to be seen here. He tucked the man's arm under his own and began walking them both away, ducking into Aunt Peggy's and then up Old Maids Lane to the inn at the top of the hill. "A captain?"

Josh ducked his head and lied with the ease of long practice, "I was looking for a pretty strumpet to celebrate with when I saw the fire."

"Do you think it *was* the molly house of which Reverend Jenson spoke?" Robinson asked with a naivety that made Josh glad he had lied. "I thought it was a gambling den!"

"If it was, I'm still not sure how Christian it was to burn that man alive." Some of the nagging sense of injustice made its way unwisely out in that remark.

But Adam stopped on the steps of the inn and said, "You're right. I had not thought it, but to excuse murder in the service of God, well... It's not what I was taught at my mother's knee."

"Indeed."

The inn had been built in a native style, with many pillars and balconies. Cool air from the sea swept up into it, and the flagged floors were almost chill at this early hour. Josh's shouting for service brought out a yawning young woman from the kitchen, who looked at their soot stained faces and gave them a brilliant white smile, amused to see them looking as black as she was herself.

Later, washed and with the smoke brushed from their coats, they sat down to a meal of gammon and eggs, slabs of white bread spread with new butter, and ale drawn up cool from the cellar. Josh drank more than he ate, the beer soothing a throat he had not realized was so raw. But Robinson ate like a man starving and eyed what he could not eat with regret.

"So," he said, when at last he could not fit another

mouthful in, "captain, eh?"

"In truth, only 'master and commander'," Josh clarified and found that—contrary to what might be expected—the inner pain hurt more now that the outer man was satisfied and at rest. "The *Macedonian* was bought into the service yesterday, and I am named her commander until someone more appropriate may be found. Or I prove myself beyond doubt—which ever comes first."

"Is that not extraordinarily rapid advancement?" said Adam, wiping his fingers with the tablecloth and looking away, down the hill to where the flat roof of the Summersgill house was visible, spiky palms and orange trees in pots on top of it, glowing against the sky. "Fortune smiles on you."

"It is Captain Kenyon's doing." Josh too looked down; to the small lodging house from which Peter had now removed himself. Peter's small terraced house was on the other side of St. George, and though it was less than five minutes walk away, it could have been the other side of the world. Josh had taken Mrs. Hodges' larger room despite everything, on the understanding that he could keep his own mattress. But already, less than a week later, the scent of Peter had faded from it, until he had to burrow into its center and draw the sheet over his head before he could catch the elusive comfort of it and fall asleep.

He looked back at the time before Kenyon, before love, as an age of innocence lost. It had all been so much easier then.

"He recommended me."

"And Captain Kenyon's voice is very much heeded where ever he should choose to speak," said Adam. It was a shock to Josh to find that the young merchant could be resentful, too, like reaching out to a fluffy pet dog, only to have it close its teeth on your fingers.

"Captain Kenyon has been a true friend to me," Josh said stiffly. "I was a midshipman with no prospects when we met, and through his influence I now have my own ship. I'm a poor Irishman with no family, and I'm fortunate to have acquired such a patron."

All of which was, of course, quite true and did not make one whit of difference. It should have been a comfort to retain Peter's friendship, but Josh was finding it difficult, at present, for every mention of the man was another tug on the hook and line that seemed to have embedded themselves in his chest, and he could not ask people to stop mentioning Peter while still feigning to be friends.

Josh took a few swigs of his beer, and that eased the constriction in his throat enough so that he could lean forward and say, "May I speak to you frankly, Mr. Robinson?"

"If you want me to stand aside, so that your friend may have unimpeded access to Miss Jones," said Robinson bitterly, pushing back his blond curls and scattering a small shower of soot on the table, "you have wasted your breakfast. I have already said goodbye to her, I must presume, for the last time."

Josh's heart fell. He told himself—again—that he was doing this from sheer disinterested friendship, but—again— he failed to convince himself. "You misunderstand me entirely, Mr. Robinson. To begin with, I know what it is to be hungry, and I know what it is to be in love with no hope of a return. I'm not trying to buy you off. I'm trying to help."

"Why? Why would you help me against your friend's interests when, as you say, you owe him so much?"

It was the question Josh had been asking himself since he saw Adam at the foot of the burning stairs; he could only give it the same answer. "Because I think you love her, and that she loves you. And Peter—he's flattered by her notice; he thinks she'd be *suitable*, but his heart is no more engaged with her than it would be with any other prize. You know I value him above all other men on this earth? You know I

128

owe him everything? So, as his friend, I can say that the man is a blind fool to think she cares for him, and in my opinion, he deserves better than a wife who accepts him as a grudging second best, only to cuckold him at the first chance with the man she truly loves."

Adam threw down his knife with an angry clatter, half rose from his seat. "You impugn her honor if you think she would ever...!"

And Josh rose too, facing him down, eye to eye. "That's not the point, and you know it. Christ, man! Tell me why you've given up? If I were in your position, I'd be fighting still for what was *mine* by right! I don't understand you!"

While they had been eating, the room had filled, and there was now a general disapproving rustling of papers to indicate they had stepped too far for politeness and should either call for their pistols or back down. Choosing the latter, Adam sank back into his seat and put his head in his blistered hands.

"What can I do?" he whispered. "If I had only a little money, enough to offer her a house and a single servant, I know she would take me. But I have debts in the hundreds of pounds. Last night, Captain Andrews, you found me reduced to sponging a stake from my friends and looking for a card game in the hopes of winning just enough funds to finance *one* journey that I might hazard my future upon. And I could not manage to achieve even that."

Josh wondered how far he should go with this fellow feeling. How many separate pieces of the puzzle he could afford to give Robinson before the man put the evidence together and condemned him. But it felt good to be able to alleviate someone's misery, to change a fate so like his own. "Is that all?" he said. Calling for the kitchen maid to bring him pen and paper he wrote down an address and a few words of recommendation.

"Take this to the timber factory on Penno's Wharf and ask to speak to Mr. Jack Clarkson. He runs a highly successful timber and fur business and is always looking for more ships. If you mention my name, I'm sure he will be delighted to finance a voyage, for the usual commission, of course."

Mr. Jack Clarkson was another man Josh had known from Mother Clap's molly house in London. The constant threat, the need to identify allies, to know where to run to in case of exposure had ingrained in him the habit of keeping track of such contacts. Though he was reluctant to use them except in great need, he soothed his doubts by telling himself that Adam's need was great enough. Clarkson himself might see it more in the light of Josh putting fresh business his way rather than a request for help. And should Adam ever find out about his employer's vice, and somehow connect that with Josh in his mind, it was always possible that obligation and gratitude would keep him silent.

It was certainly a less ridiculously suicidal thing to do than to decide to visit St. George's only molly house while the repercussions of Reverend Jenson's sermon were still roaring around the town. If Josh had not particularly cared about his survival then, why should he do so now?

He picked up the piece of paper with address and introduction on it, and offered it to Robinson, who took it with all the awe suitable for handling a new hope. Adam read it, shocked, disbelieving. "He will take me on? Give my men a wage? And me?"

"Yes, for my sake. He is a...reclusive, private sort of man; you must promise not to press him or pry for more than he is willing to tell you."

"Oh!" There was a small moment of revelation on a face that had become so radiant it might have modeled for a Greek statue, had it been a little less thin, and Josh realized that Adam thought he had been put in contact with a smuggler and was willing to keep silence about it. It might not actually be that far from the truth. Josh had taken care never to inquire.

"Captain Andrews!" said Robinson, rising and shaking Josh's hand. "I... God's blood, sir, you are a messenger of Providence. Your kindness leaves me unable to speak, but if the prayers of two loving souls now given new hope are of any practical benefit, you will be showered with blessings. What may I do to repay you? I can scarcely restrain myself from flying out the door and running all the way there now, but tell me first what your dearest wish is, so that should ever the chance come my way, I can return to you the hundredth part of this obligation."

Despite everything, Josh could not help laughing at this enthusiasm. It did help—and not at all, he told himself, just because it delayed the inevitable day when Peter wed and was out of his reach forever.

"I need nothing, sir," he said. "Pray do not trouble yourself in the slightest. But cherish a little more kindness for Captain Kenyon in future, perhaps. For my sake."

As Josh stood at the Inn's door, watching Adam run down the steep hill like a deer, all slender, gaunt grace and legs, another small dot came toiling up the road towards him. Within five minutes it had resolved itself into the youngest of his new midshipmen, Hal Tucker, hatless and coatless, scarlet as a tomato and breathing like a bellows.

"Please, sir...I've been...looking for you...everywhere. Commodore wants you, sir, half an hour ago."

Chapter Seventeen

Commodore Dalby's office was small and filled to bursting with three captains and the commodore himself. The commodore, trying to unroll a large map on the small deal table looked up with a grunt when Josh entered. Josh bowed, to him, to Peter, and to Captain Joslyn of the *Asp*.

"*Macedonian* ready to sail, Andrews?"

"Yes, sir."

"Good." Dalby looked down again. "We've received a report of a French ship of the line—possibly the *Indomitable*—cruising up the coast of America. She has not come to the aid of any of the French privateers nor has she taken part in any action against British troops on the ground. I've also had reports of strange sail from Fort Albany. Call it an intuition, but I suspect the French are trying to take advantage of our distraction in order to break the treaty and retake Hudson Bay.

"The three of you should be a match for a three-decker. You'll proceed to Hudson Bay in company with and under the command of Post Captain Joslyn and deal with whatever you find there. Understood?"

"Understood, sir."

"Sail ho!" came the cry from the masthead. Peter ran up the shrouds, glass in hand, to the maintop, looked where the midshipman pointed, and could see, perhaps, a smudge of white too regular for a cloud. Excitement coursing through him, he came down to universal smiles on deck.

"Make the signal for Captain Joslyn!" he commanded, and waited until the signal flag was flying before returning his attention to the sea.

"And prepare to tack ship!"

"Aye aye, sir!"

As they came about, Peter saw flags break out on the *Asp*, signaling a general pursuit. He bent on as much sail as the rigging would safely bear, and after an hour, it became clear that the *Seahorse* was gaining on the unknown sail.

By the following day, they had gained ten miles and could see her quite clearly, green hull banded with cheerful yellow. The name painted on her stern was *Virginie*, a thirty-two, a little heavier than the *Macedonian*. She was flying a Dutch flag, but apart from the sheer implausibility of this, the coxswain's mate recognized her as the thirty-two which had taken him prisoner in the year sixty-seven, and had then been under Captain Jean-Paul deBourne, a gentleman of the old school.

"Sir," said Peter's first lieutenant, the newly senior Mr. Howe, "that's the Hudson Strait ahead, sir. If we don't do something now, and there *is* a three-decker in the bay, well, our prospects will be considerably worse."

The man affected Peter like a bad smell—quite unfairly, for he was a competent officer, and this was a justified worry that Peter shared. He supposed it was just that he was used to Andrews there, with whom he would have shared his thoughts, and the knowledge that Andrews was on his own ship, inaccessible, made his rigid back ache.

"Mr. Howe, I suppose it has not occurred to you that I might have already thought of this? Nor that your asking the question is disrespectful in the utmost to Captain Joslyn, who can be supposed to have thought of this, too?"

"No, sir, sorry, sir," said Howe, rubbing a hand over the

cocoa-brown stubble on his chin and looking cowed.

Worried that he might be turning into a monster of authority like Walker, Peter relented. "However, I think we can begin putting things in train for action. We won't clear until we're given the order, but there will be no harm in putting out the fearnought screens and slow-match now."

"Aye aye, sir." Howe smiled and hurried away. Feeling the need for something to counterbalance his presence, Peter took out his glass and trained it on the *Macedonian*, watching the small figure of her captain on his own quarterdeck. He had left off the expensive and prestigious wig, and in the red tinged sunset light, his own hair shone like a point of fire. Peter, admiring both ship and man, huddled into his greatcoat, and felt briefly piercingly happy. Andrews at his right hand and a steady colleague at his left, a battle ahead, and the sun going down in a sheet of flame over a blue shadow of land. There was a smell of slow-match in the air, and all the world seemed eager, poised for glory.

Life, he thought, did not get much better than this, and at the thought some presentiment of danger made him reach out and stroke the *Seahorse*'s rail, touching wood.

The signal to engage broke out on the *Asp* and time for reflection was over. On deck the cannons were set loose, and there was a rumbling below as the larger thirty-eight pounders were brought into action on the gun deck. Ship's boys ran up from the armory with canisters of shot and powder, and the swivel guns at the bow were already shotted and primed.

"All divisions ready, sir," Howe reported, returning like an unwanted guest.

"Bow chasers fire at will," Peter commanded, "and a guinea for the man who shoots out the first sail."

The swivels barked with a high pitched note, like terriers, and the crews of the cannon tied up their hair with their scarves, spat on their hands. *Seahorse* plunged through the smoke and the cold arctic air was briefly warm and thick, smelling of gunpowder.

But the *Virginie,* had been lying to them about her speed. Now her captain trimmed the yards, she filled, and staysails broke out on all masts, spritsail and spritsail topsail on her boom. At once she leaped forward out of range. Peter ordered staysails set himself, and royals, touching the braces of the masts to feel whether they would take it. To starboard, the *Macedonian* came up beside them, her more powerful chasers firing. A ball hit the *Virginie*'s stern galley and a spray of glass leaped up, glittering. A little closer and—though they could not rake her with a broadside—they might keep up a steady fire with the swivels, sending shot the whole unprotected length of her deck.

No, not unprotected, for now the *Virginie's* stern chasers spoke—there was a yellow cloud of smoke and a roar. He felt the wind as the ball passed his elbow, made a hole in the hammock netting behind him, and he laughed, feeling all earthly cares depart at the nearness of death.

"Like that, is it?"

Looking back, he saw that the burst of speed was leaving the *Asp* behind, and he wondered why *Virginie* had not done this at the start, but had deliberately allowed the fourth rate to keep up. Was she that confident that the three-decker she undoubtedly believed he knew nothing about would be enough to take on three British warships? Well, it was time to disabuse her of that notion, he'd take on the *Virginie* and the *Indomitable,* too, if he had to.

The wind remained constant. Peter gave the order for the studding-sails to be set, just as the *Virginie* began her turn into Hudson Straight. The speed cracked on; they were sailing now at thirteen knots straight towards *Virginie*'s turned broadside, and the French captain took the opportunity to open a full roaring fire, raking the *Seahorse* from stem to stern. The air was full of metal. One of the gun crew, receiving a ball in the breast, was literally burst apart and his limbs landed on either side of the boat, his severed head catching in the splinter netting and hanging there.

The men on deck flung themselves flat on the boards, including Midshipman Prendergast, a boy of thirteen, for whom this was his first experience of battle.

Peter walked over to the boy, acutely conscious that the gun crews on the *Virginie* were reloading and that the second broadside would be closer, more deadly, as the strip of water between the vessels narrowed. "Stand up, Mr. Prendergast," he said firmly. "A gentleman does not cower." He took the boy by the elbow, feeling the racking shudders of fear, and stood him on his feet, with a smile. Then he leaned forward and whispered the words his own captain had told him on a similar occasion, long ago. "If you cannot be brave, it is perfectly adequate to pretend. But pretend you must. How would the men feel otherwise, seeing their officers afraid?"

The boy gave him a waxy smile in return and nodded. Then he was promptly sick into his hat. Choosing not to notice, Peter said, "Get someone to clear Beatty's head from the netting, would you? Assemble what pieces you can find for burial," and walked up the quarterdeck stairs just as the second wave of iron smashed into the *Seahorse* and came shrieking and smoking down her deck. The main mast was hit a jarring blow, splinters flew through the air, humming like bees. Peter saw that the *Macedonian* had begun to turn, but in the process had lost way. A shot from her chasers knocked off the boom of the *Virginie's* mizzen spanker, and the whole fell, tangled to the deck.

For one instant her stern was to the *Seahorse's* broadside, and Peter scarcely had to shout "fire" before all the weight of metal his small sloop possessed was loosed on the *Virginie* but at the speed they were going, he could only fire once before she had gone racing into Hudson Straight, and he had to go about to avoid being driven into Resolution Island.

This was easier said than done, with the land so close on his lee. In the end he had to club-haul to gain enough sea room to double back, set all sail once more and drive through, almost close enough to pick the little slipper orchids on Cape Chidley's grassy point.

By that time the night was black as the inside of a barrel, and he shortened sail to avoid driving her onto some unknown reef in the dark.

It had never been such a struggle to avoid looking worried, and he was almost inclined to kick the ship's cat when the lookout spotted lanterns, and they eased gently to a halt in the shelter of Akpatok Island, where the unwounded *Macedonian* had dropped anchor for the night.

He dined with Andrews in a strange state of fear and lust, barely able to give sensible answers to Josh's questions. "Do you think we should wait for the Asp? Do you think it was an ambush—I thought so myself and decided not to try a night pursuit... Are you feeling quite alright?"

"When I thought you had gone on ahead without me," Peter said, quite forgetting the servants who stood behind their chairs, "my heart failed within me. I thought we were ruined for sure."

"Then we'll wait for the *Asp*," said Josh, giving him a look of warning and a kick beneath the table that gave him the only injury of the battle.

Noon saw the *Asp* rounding the point, with Joslyn alternately shamefaced and indignant—for missing the skirmish, and for them leaving him behind. For the next week they proceeded in convoy and entered the great bay itself without a sight of their prey.

It gnawed at Josh to think he had had the enemy in his sight and let him get away. In a somewhat different way, Peter's dazed vulnerability gnawed at him, too, and the dreams he had had on the *Nimrod*, before all this started, returned, all the more explicit for experience. It was, therefore, with a madness of relief that just as they were passing the Sleeper Islands he heard the lookout exclaim "Strange sail sir, two I think, sou', sou'-west!"

"Now we'll show 'em, eh, sir?" said his first, Tom Dench, with an eager look, and Josh who was desperate to give his mind something to do, other than to go on playing over last week's solitary dinner, laughed.

"Damn right. You may clear for action."

With the *Indomitable* at her side, the *Virginie* fled no more. The two French ships set sail towards him, and the vast majesty of the three-decker was like a storm-cloud bearing down.

His intent was to lay alongside the *Virginie* and board if he could. Fight his way through her, take her and leave the *Indomitable* for Peter and Joslyn. Peeling off from the convoy, he headed upwind, to gain the weather gage, so that he could run down at the *Virginie* and force her into her protector, using her as a shield against the three-decker's vast weight of armaments.

But as he did so, fully concentrating on the two vessels ahead, there came a booming series of retorts from astern. Looking back, he saw three more French vessels—a ship and two brigs—slip from their concealed anchorages behind the Sleeper Islands and make for the *Asp*. They were the *Aimable*, little less than the *Asp*'s tonnage and better gunned, along with the *Gloire* and the *Trounin*, of fourteen guns and a hundred men apiece.

He saw the *Asp* and the *Aimable* lying side by side, their broadsides hammering at one another, while the *Gloire* raked the British ship from the stern and the *Trounin* hemmed her in to leeward, with a slow, measured fire at her masts, saw Peter break from pursuit of the *Indomitable* to go back to the *Asp*'s aid, and laughed. Laughed long and hard because it was his first action as a captain, and he already knew he would not come out of it alive. Whether it was an impromptu trap or a long laid one, they had run their necks into it good and proper, and he, furthest in, had no chance at all at fighting his way back out to bring the news back to the commodore.

But Peter might. Peter or Joslyn—they were closer to the bay's entrance. Peter, in his fast little sloop might seem unimportant to the French commander, in the same way that the *Trounin* and the *Gloire* were insignificant alone. If he broke for it, he might yet get away.

But not with the *Indomitable* on his tail, and certainly not with the swift, well sailed *Virginie*. He laughed again, sliding down the backstay onto the deck like a boy skylarking, and everything seemed clear to him, in a moment of battle vision that took him back to the tradition of his Fenian ancestors. The purpose of his life—the reason he had been born, already condemned to flame, and then allowed to love.

"It seems that in going after the *Gloire* they've left the glory to us," he said to young Hal, who was looking at him with the careful awe reserved for the mad. "Set all possible sail to intercept the man of war. They're going to be talking about this in France into the next century."

"Aye, sir!"

"And then the crew are to get in the boats and flee to shore."

"Sir!" Lt. Dench drew himself up in protest. He was a long term sailor fated to serve under young idiots and to try and teach them their duties. "We can't win, but there's no shame in surrender."

"Get the lads to the boats, please, Lieutenant. And then you may set me a fire in the hold. I'll man the helm myself."

"Sir," said Dench, looking as though his dog had died, "please, sir, you don't have to..."

"My mind is quite made up," said Josh and smiled.

139

"Give my regards to Commodore Dalby when you see him again, and my will is in the right hand drawer of my writing slope in my lodgings. Good luck to you."

Peter had come alongside the *Gloire*. Caught in the crossfire between the *Seahorse* and the *Asp* the little brig was being scientifically taken apart. Blood poured from her scuppers and painted her black sides crimson, staining the sea beneath her. He had shot away the rudder, and when the main mast fell, leaving her without the ability to get under way or to steer, he left her wallowing, bore up and began to do the same to the *Trounin*.

In the pause, when he cast off the boarding cables that held *Gloire* close so that *Seahorse*'s guns could do maximum damage, he could hear the deeper roar of the *Asp*'s guns, the answering bellow of the *Aimable*. *Aimable*'s broadsides were heavier but less rapid and less well aimed. *Asp*, with her mizzen mast trailing like an anchor in the sea and her own pouring spouts of blood still seemed to his eye to be holding her own.

Now he pushed away from the *Gloire*, and barely able to find a wind, he used the *Asp*'s side to pull the *Seahorse* around and creep up upon the *Trounin* like a snail.

But the *Trounin* was fresh—from her position on the *Asp*'s stern she had suffered only a little bruising from the stern chasers, and the nine great guns of her starboard side began a lively battering of Peter's poor ship—already more than half a hulk, tattered sails strewn over her cannons and the corpses of her men.

"Sir, they're saying it's hopeless!" Lt. Howe cried, loud enough to be heard from heads to stern gallery. "Even if we take the *Aimable*, how will we ever stand against the three-decker? They're saying it's being held in reserve to crush us when we've used our last strength here."

"Are they indeed?" he said, wishing that for once he

could act like a common tar and punch the stupid man in the mouth. "Well you may tell them that it's possible the *Indomitable may* take us, but it's *certain* that I shall shoot the first man who leaves his post myself."

A roar and a crash, and for a moment he had no idea what had happened, until Howe leaned forward and plucked the oak splinter—a foot and a half long—out of his side. A brief wave of dizziness went over Peter but then, with a ponderous, grating slide, the *Asp* seemed to shake herself and glide gently forwards. When the *Aimable* tried to follow, her one standing mast bent under the strain of sail, and the backstays parted. The great, six ton timber came crashing down upon her men, and upon the *Seahorse*'s head, driving it under the waves. Seas began pouring aboard, and as the *Trounin*'s gunners kept up a relentless fire, the *Seahorse*'s men abandoned their cannon to shift the dead weight before it sank the ship.

Thus tangled, Peter saw the *Asp* make sail, getting away. He wished Joslyn well, hoped he would escape with news of this unexpected fleet, this French occupation of what was, by treaty, British land. Only how would the *Asp* escape the *Indomitable*, which had been hanging back all this time, waiting to strike only if it proved necessary to do so?

The next few moments were taken up with the capstan, rigging ropes around the *Aimable*'s mast and slowly winching it off the deck—the piper piping all the while, the men huffing shanties as they pushed at the long levers, and shot screaming aboard from both French ships.

There was a strange light in the smoke, like the rising of a sun, and at the same time, a knocking on the sides of the ship as British seamen began to come aboard up the main chains. "Sir! Sir!"

They were the *Macedonian*'s men, some of them still with the jaunty straw hats and the ships name embroidered in glinting gold on the ribbon.

"Just you watch, sir. Just you watch!"

"The water is above the cable tier, sir," said Howe quietly, catching something of their awe. "And still gaining. If we don't send men to the pumps now, we will sink within the next quarter of an hour."

And sending men to the pumps would mean abandoning the guns. Would mean...

But he couldn't fail. He had never failed; it wasn't in his nature. Peter Kenyon did not...

The wind, blowing the *Trounin*'s smoke back over it, briefly cleared a patch of brilliant sea, and he saw it all with minute clarity—the *Macedonian* in flames, driving into the *Indomitable*'s bowsprit. Her sails were sheets of fire, and her decks blacker than pitch. The *Indomitable*'s rested, eager crew were trying to fend her off with oars and poles but the wind drove her back each time. If he squinted his streaming eyes, Peter could imagine the figure at the helm, holding it steady, not letting them brush off this kiss of death. And then flame leaped the gap, the *Indomitable* was on fire too.

"Oh, my God, please, no!" he said, and something cracked deep inside the *Macedonian*'s hull. Her masts flew into the air like the stems of rockets and a white sphere of fire too intense to watch pushed out of her, bursting her into tumbling, jagged shards, blowing a hole in the *Indomitable* large enough to row a captain's barge inside.

The *Indomitable* tilted, men flinging themselves off her into the sea, tilted again, filled with water and sank. There was nothing left of the *Macedonian* at all but strewed wreckage. Peter pressed his hand to his side, where the blood from his wound was making his shirt feel uncomfortably cold, and staggered, fighting for breath, for sense, for the right words.

"Strike our colors," he said at last in a small, dead voice. Yes, dead—Josh was dead, so what did it matter? "Tell them we surrender."

Chapter Eighteen

"Well, Captain, you will give me your parole and be free as a guest in my house, or not, and spend the summer down in a jail cell. It's your choice, I don't very much mind either way."

The destruction of the *Indomitable* had caused feelings to run high in the French fleet. A three-decker, she had gone to the bottom with over a thousand men onboard, broaching to in seconds, and though all the ships on the bay had been pouring with the blood of the dead, Peter could understand the horror. To sink with no hope of quarter, it was not one of the accepted risks of the game.

As a result of Josh's ferocious action, Captain Duarte of the *Aimable*, expecting a counter strike as soon as Commodore Dalby could send one from Bermuda, and with considerably fewer working vessels to meet it, did not feel confident of his ability to keep his prisoners alive during the long journey back to France, where they would be incarcerated until they could be exchanged for French prisoners of equal value. He had therefore sailed to Boston and pressed them upon his unsuspecting American allies.

It was in the back of Peter's mind that he should refuse to give his parole. He should be working, even now, to escape and return home. But something had broken in him, and he was not certain even what it was, let alone how to mend it.

"Mr. Ward," he said, when the silence had grown so deep they could both hear the cries of the dockers in the harbor, "I give you my word as an officer and a gentleman that I will not attempt to escape until I am released, either by fair exchange or by the end of the war."

"Can't say fairer than that," said Ward, a portly, businesslike man, who seemed to have come in for this duty by virtue of having a large house and a French wife who wrote revolutionary pamphlets. Peter suspected the duty was little to his liking, and the relief at not having to turn jailer was apparent on Ward's round red apple of a face.

"May I write to my friends in Bermuda?" he said after another pause in which both men felt they should be saying something but neither knew what. "I...there is unhappy news to tell to many, which I would wish them to hear from a more sympathetic source than the naval gazette."

His calm began to fracture at that sentence; he could feel the cracks spreading out from it, as they spread from an incautious foot stepped on thin ice. He was fragile at present, but beneath him the cracks were widening above the plunge into icy depths. He tried to ease away from the flaw but could not. It spread and spread beneath him, and he tensed for the sudden final break.

"Of course. Just go on into the drawing room; I'll have Nancy bring you paper. I heard about the fight, of course. Don't let my wife hear me say this," he shook his head at the thought, his eyes shining, "but that must have been something! A French ship of the line and a little, tiny thirty-two? Hoo! I don't mean to be unpatriotic, but that was a brave man."

"Yes." Peter was startled into a small smile, "Yes, he was. He was my particular friend, but I had no idea he intended anything so rash or so...so glorious."

"Your friend, was he?" Ward rocked back on his heels. He wore no wig, so to Peter he seemed always informal, but the look in his pale eyes was unmistakably kind. "Well then,

144

I won't say that all this could have been avoided if Westminster had chosen to treat with us like civilized men. How they ever thought they could beat us into submission is probably as much a mystery to you as it is to me. So go and write your letters, son, and mourn your dead. You won't be the only man doing the same."

As Peter worked his way through the letters of condolence, his handwriting growing progressively shakier as his own grief insinuated itself under his guard, he considered the justice of this rebuke. He had never failed in anything, and yet when had he ever done anything but what was expected of him? He had great sympathy for the colonist's desire for self rule, but when had he ever said so? When had he ever stood up for those things that really meant something to him? He had not. He had chosen always do to what everyone else thought was right, not what his own heart told him.

And in doing so—he put the pen down, rubbed his stinging eyes, telling himself it was fatigue that made them burn—he had rejected the one thing in his life that had ever made him completely happy.

He looked out at the sea, the ships in the harbor visible and yet so far away and wondered if he could pray. He wanted to pray, "Oh, God, *please,* don't let him have done this because of me, because I hurt him, because I put an end to something that *he* said must end."

Pulling a fresh sheet of paper towards himself he took up the pen again and began to write *My dear Mr. Summersgill, I am happy to inform you that I am alive and well, though confined. I am under house arrest in the dwelling of a worthy gentleman of Boston named Mr. Ward. I am quite comfortable and lack nothing but my freedom.*

I am including here my wish that you should have power of attorney over my small estate in Bermuda and beg leave

145

to ask you to see that my servants are paid and are not in distress in my absence.

Peter wondered if he should express some conventional sentiments of attachment to Emily, but his disordered thoughts rose up against such base hypocrisy. When the world lay at his feet it had seemed natural that every prize should be his, but now he wondered if she even liked him, and more, he wondered if—beyond a basic physical appreciation of her charms—he even liked her. How much did he know about her? Not half so much as he had known about Josh, and he had cared not half so much to know.

Please pass on my love to my mother, and the reassurance that I am as well as it is possible to be, though I may not be able to send her the bird of paradise feathers she asked for in her last. My regards to Emily, and I remain, sir,

Your most obliged servant,
Peter Alexander Kenyon.

Folding up this last letter and sealing it left him finally with nothing to do. He bowed his head into his hands and closed his eyes. He wanted to pray, "Please, tell him I loved him," but he was not sure God would allow him such a prayer. Suicide and sodomite, was Joshua Andrews even now in Hell? If he was, what then? What then became of all the things Peter had fought for? If God himself was an unjust tyrant, and the navy only an instrument of oppression, and good and love not possible in the world, not worth striving or fighting for, what then was the point of being Peter Kenyon? What then was the point of anything?

Chapter Nineteen

Josh was in Hell. He could see the blood pulse scalding through his closed eyelids, feel his skin tighten beneath the licking flames. When he breathed the air was molten lead; when he tried not to, he smothered and panic forced him to open his mouth and gasp the boiling metal once more.

There had been flames and then cold, striking to his heart like a lance of ice. Then darkness. Now Hell tossed like a boat on rough water, and his voice shocked him, as agony tore the outcry from him unwillingly.

Voices spoke above his head—a man and a woman—but he could not understand the language. There was a pleasant, rhythmic noise, accompanied by the drip of water and a large rustling full of bird-song. Then small hands pulled him into a sitting position, spread something cool on his achingly tight, tender face, and he found himself cradled in a woman's embrace. "Sleep," she said, her voice full of tenderness. "You are safe."

He thought of his mother and of the gentleness of Irish skies, gray as an arch of pearl. He fell asleep again, yearning for a day of long, cool Irish rain.

When next he woke, he was being lifted out of the boat onto the bank. There were male arms about him and his head lolled against a strong shoulder. With great labor he managed to haul up his eyelids for a moment, to find his face nestled into another man's neck, cushioned by a long fall of ebony hair, glossy and soft.

"Peter," he said, for there couldn't be two men with hair so fine and dark. "Oh, Peter, thank God!" and he clung and wept like an infant, in some hinterland of the spirit well beyond pain and dignity. Closing his aching eyes again he set his mouth to Peter's neck, in something between a kiss and a baby's instinctive need for its mother's skin, then drew back, puzzled and afraid. The smell was wrong. Peter smelled of pomade, wig powder, ink and steel, a smell he thought the best thing in the world, but this man smelled of leather and other scents, unknown and disturbing.

He opened his eyes again, drew back and met the surprised look of a young man the color of baked terracotta, with dark, dark eyes as beautiful as his hair. "Mother of God!" Josh whispered. Then the young man gave a broad grin that did not suit his sullen good looks and carried Josh over a short scramble to his camp, setting him down gently on a mattress of spruce branches, covered with furs. Trying to work out what this meant—that he was not dead, that he was not captured by the French, that he was, perhaps, captured by some tribe of Indians who wanted him for God knows what, Josh fell asleep again.

"Come, you should eat." Shaken awake, he found the sky had been blocked out by a tent of leather, and his captor? savior? host? stood before him with a bowl in his hand. Behind his shoulder, a young woman sat, babe at her breast, composedly stirring the pot over the fire and looking on with interest.

"You speak English," Josh said stupidly, while trying to work out a way of sitting up which did not result in him fainting from the pain. After watching this struggle for a while, the man put his bowl down, sat on the edge of the bed and lifted Josh into his arms once more. Josh managed to get a grip on the bowl, but could not get his sore, swollen fingers to close on the spoon.

"I am not feeding you," said the young man, a smile in his voice. "If you are baby enough to need it, I'm sure Opichi will do it, when she is finished with our other child."

Josh laughed, coughed, tasting the smoke in his lungs, and sipped from the bowl. It was a stew of rice and fish, flavored with some yellow meal he did not recognize, and the taste seemed to pour new life into him, waking body and spirit together. "Thank you," he said, and—exhausted by the effort—lay back limply against the man behind him, who put the uneaten food back on the ground and ran his fingers through Josh's hair, startling him into sitting upright again.

It was Josh's turn now to look at his host with wide, inquiring eyes. The man chuckled, put his hand on his heart, and said "Giniw."

It was at once so commonplace a thing to do—to make introductions—and yet so intimate that Josh's anxiety could not compete with it. "Giniw?" he leaned back again, letting his hands rest on the arms that carefully tightened around him. It was so nice to be held, to be kept safe and supported by someone else's strength, and this was innocent enough, wasn't it? With the man's wife looking on, there could be nothing more to it than the joy of simple human comfort. "I'm Joshua."

At first, Opichi would dress his burns, but soon she passed the task to Giniw and began a long, arduous business of tanning a whole deer hide. Watching her work, the baby on her back, or tucked beside her in a cradle, where she could snatch moments to amuse it before turning back to the hard labor he began to feel like something of a cuckoo in the nest. Giniw took to the task of looking after him with enthusiasm, and Josh in turn grew to rely on that hour when Giniw's large, cool hands would smooth the ointment over his face and neck, shoulders and chest, as the best hour in the day. Though he did not have enough generosity in him to put a stop to it, he felt as guilty as any wife could desire.

In the third week, Giniw declared that he was going hunting and disappeared into the woods, leaving Josh and Opichi alone. It took only an hour, during which he watched her feed and change the baby, chop wood, fetch water, attempt three times to return to her tanning project, only to be interrupted by the child crying, take out a birch box of rice, spill it on the floor, and burst into tears of sheer exhaustion to make him drag his splinted legs out of bed and—gingerly, haltingly—fumble his way through putting a pan of swamp tea on the fire. When he had gathered himself from that exertion, panting as though he had run a mile, he picked up the crying child—watching for permission—and amused her as well as he could with the shiny silver locket he wore around his neck.

Opichi burst into a further fit of tears at the sight, then, when the flashing, twirling bauble had kept her daughter silent for five minutes, she laughed, braided back her hair, and poured the tea.

"You didn't need to be burdened with an extra child," he said, thrown back with shocking familiarity to his own childhood, to remembered scenes of his mother—apron over her head—rocking in silent tears in the center of the brawl of children and need. His mother had not let him help her. Woe betide the thought of his father coming home and finding him doing women's work! But he recognized the symptoms and wondered what it meant that she would show it to him, when she had remained so stoic and so capable while Giniw was present.

"When we found you washed to shore among the clams," she said after they had drunk, "we recognized your uniform. Giniw knew that the colonists were fighting the British because your Great Father had said the white man could take no more of our land. He knew the French were on the colonists' side—against us—even though the French were once our friends. And so, Giniw said, we should do what we could to help you because your cause is our cause."

She looked at Josh sideways, with a twist of mischievous smile that even Josh could see was dazzling. "But I think his heart spoke louder than his head, even then."

The baby was now soothing her teething pains by chewing on Josh's finger, so he covered the guilty start by looking down on her fuzzy head and telling her about it, in a bout of baby talk that left the child unmoved but the mother in stitches.

Sadly the distraction did not work for longer than it took Opichi to get her breath back. "You cannot tell me you have not noticed he desires you. Nor have you been exactly discouraging towards him."

Josh was not sure he had ever been more embarrassed in his entire life. "I'm sorry," he said, conscious of how wretched he was, how unwashed, crippled, and pathetic. "I don't mean anything by it. I was just born this way—wrong inside. You can't know—when I thought I was going to die, it was *wonderful*. I thought I'd finally got beyond it. I thought that would be the last of it. And then I get given a second life, and I still can't *stop*. I'm sorry. I didn't have the strength to hide it. But I will. I will now."

Opichi drank her tea and looked away, frowning, then she came and sat down close to him, laying a careful hand on his wrist where the burns were beginning to fade into his normal pallor. "Joshua," she asked, "why do you say that you are wrong? You are what the Creator made you to be, and he made all things good."

This observation stopped Josh's guilt and self-hatred in its tracks, for didn't the Bible say the same thing? He touched the thought gingerly; it almost hurt to contemplate the possibility that God had made him this way because it was a good way to be.

"Among our people," Opichi smiled at his stunned look, "the *agokwa* are honored. We say they have the spirit of both men and women in themselves, and so they see clearer. They see all the way around. Many of our healers and our holy men are like you."

She laughed. "Giniw thought you were an *agokwa* when you wept on his neck like a woman, but I had never heard that the British had *agokwa*, so I said you could not be. But I think after all that I was wrong. I do not know if a man would have known, as you did, what was in my heart this morning. Besides, you want Giniw. That, I am not mistaken about."

In turmoil, Josh did not know which part of this to answer first. Even in the middle of his slowly stirring joy he had time for a stab of anger at being told that he was not a man. Being something different—something so foreign that English did not have a word for it—could not but feel like a rebuke, no matter how she softened it.

"You are not appalled?"

She laughed again and gave him a swift, light hug that left him bemused but smiling. "Of course you want him," she said, "he is beautiful. You are beautiful, too, in a strange way—it is only natural he should want you. And I have been asking him, ever since I felt heavy with child, to take another wife. Someone with whom I could share the work, because I am so very tired."

Putting her head to one side, she examined him carefully, her gaze lingering on the hand still cradling her daughter's head, where the baby had finally fallen asleep in his lap. "We are thinking it would be a good idea for him to marry you."

Chapter Twenty

"Sir," said Emily quietly, looking up from the letter to see her father's face looking old and stricken, "may I tell this to Mr. Robinson?" She saw the denial—the bitterness of a man who thinks his grief is being taken advantage of—and hurried to explain. "He has just returned from a voyage to these very shores. He has a ship and acquaintance in those parts. He could...we could offer to pay a ransom for Captain Kenyon. I will not conceal from you, Father, that the captain is not particularly dear to me, but I know he is dear to you."

"I had hoped you were finally becoming sensible of his merits," her father said, taking off his reading glasses and putting them carefully down on the writing shelf of his bureau. Trying not to resent this lack of confidence in her steadfastness, Emily took his distance glasses from her reticule and handed them to him.

"I see his merits, sir," she said with restraint, "but they are not the kind of merits which recommend themselves to me. I prefer Mr. Robinson's cheer and his humanity to Captain Kenyon's reserve and his...I beg your indulgence, but his apparent assumption that the whole world finds him praiseworthy. It is a kind of arrogance I could not bring myself to live with."

"But Mr. Robinson is so...so *slight* a man. So unfailingly pleasant. How can you be sure, my dear, he is no idle flatterer? I would be sad to see you married to a man without strength or depth—an empty cask that makes a pleasant rattling. You would soon begin to despise such a one yourself. Peter has not a particularly polished surface, I admit, but he has depth. Of Mr. Robinson's inner worth I remain unconvinced."

She took the letter from his hands and read it again, wondering how he could possibly conceive of *anyone* being passionately in love with such a cold fish as this. "But, sir, suppose Mr. Robinson did agree to this, in order to bring back the man he believes is his rival for my affections. While Captain Kenyon is gone, he might justly be hoping to amass a little wealth and ask for me himself, unopposed. Would it not sufficiently prove his moral superiority if he was to—apparently—put himself out of the race, merely because it was the right thing to do?"

Summersgill laughed at that, took his wig from its stand and put it on, disappearing into his powdering room so that his valet could properly cover it in shining white powder. "You *are* fond of the young man, aren't you? Very well, my dear, we will put him to this test, and if he passes it I will confess myself convinced."

"And we may marry?" Emily knew it was not decorous, but leaped to her feet in joy.

"If he returns with the captain, and if he can satisfy me as to his financial situation, then you may marry. But *I* will convey the request to him. If you tell him it is a test, it will be no test at all."

"My wife will have a thing or two to say to me," said Ward with a wry smile, "but I don't see why it's any less patriotic to exchange your man for money than for some prisoner who's already proved he's not capable of winning a fight." He re-opened the small chest in which Adam had brought the ransom and fingered the bank notes, the two

154

small bags of sovereigns and the rope of pearls which had been Emily's contribution.

Peter Kenyon was led into the room by a brightly liveried black boy, and Adam was shocked at the change in him. Physically he seemed quite well, but he had always walked as though the world belonged to him; his eyes had been clear as water, unburdened by self doubt or introspection of any kind. There had been a magnificence in that, as there is in the unreflective eyes of any predator, but that magnificence was gone. The man before him seemed both softer and smaller, and he thought with a stab of sudden jealousy that Emily would find the change greatly to her liking.

Kenyon gave Adam a small, wounded smile, holding out his hand. "Sir, I cannot tell you how obliged I am to you for this rescue. If there is anything I can do for you in return...?"

Adam shook the well-kept hand, and his mind conjured up by itself the moment on the *Nimrod's* deck where this situation had played out in reverse. Unwillingly, he found himself smiling back. "Captain Kenyon, you came to my aid when the privateers attacked me—I am merely returning the favor. And not only yours."

"No?"

"Your friend, Captain Andrews, put me in the way of my present prosperity and asked me to remember you kindly." Adam had mixed feelings about the man he had saved from one fire, only to plunge himself into another. A generous man, but not, perhaps, entirely stable. "So you see I am paying back a debt, rather than owed one myself."

Peter's head lifted and the worn look became sharp, full of pain. "Joshua and you?" Then the smile returned, and he ducked his head as if to throw the shadow of a tricorn over the anguish in his eyes. "I would gladly hear more about that. I...miss him."

Damn, thought Adam, not wanting to have to pity or

show compassion to his rival—a rival for whom Emily was clearly fond enough to sacrifice her favorite pearls. He wondered in what light Andrews' help for him might appear to Kenyon. How bitter it would be to learn that the last act of your best friend was to work to ruin your prospects of marriage!

But to act without pity for Kenyon at the moment would have been, to Adam's soft heart, like kicking the wounded. If resentment and revenge were required they could wait until later. Until Kenyon was once more a worthy opponent who could withstand an attack without provoking guilt. The fact that by that time he might already be married to the woman Adam loved was just another of the many ironies of the situation.

Chapter Twenty-one

The tree above him rustled its papery leaves, and sun slanted down onto Josh's bent head as he twined the willow stems together with the deftness he had learned when splicing rope. His hands were still tender, and he knew he could do better work later, when they had toughened enough, but for now it was idyllic to sit and think and work at something useful, while he tried to soak up the thought that he was not broken at all. Perhaps he never had been broken; perhaps the world in which he had grown up was merely wrong. It was taking him much longer to accept than it had taken him to learn to make baskets, but then rearranging his thinking was more intricate and more painful.

But he was making some progress, and he was so absorbed in thought and craft that he did not notice Giniw's return until the light was blocked off and his hands stilled by force. Surprised, he looked up to find Giniw watching him with that cocky grin of his, that was so like and yet so unlike Peter's unconscious arrogance—the assumption that he was master of the world—which had always made his spirit sing.

"You're back," Josh said and chided himself for once more being a specialist in the obvious.

"Yes." Giniw turned Josh's hand over and dropped into it a necklace of bone beads, each one individually carved. "I made this for you."

And once more, Josh was blindsided by something so totally unlike anything he would have expected. He stirred the little, ivory colored beads with his fingers, afraid to look up lest Giniw should despise him for being on the edge of tears. To be brought gifts like a sweetheart! Plain and open and unafraid. Permitted! He didn't know what to do. It was so...odd, when in all his life before, Peter had been the only one to treat him as though he was a friend as well as a potential fuck.

"I spoke to Opichi." Giniw had indeed a groomed and satisfied look to him that indicated he had gone to see her first and had perhaps done more than just talk. At the thought, a very unworthy stab of jealousy added itself to Josh's confusion. He didn't want to take second place any more. He didn't want to take the leftovers and be grateful to have them. If he was indeed not made wrong, why was he not entitled to as much as everyone else?

But Giniw had not followed this thought. He lifted the necklace from Josh's hand and slid it about his neck, tying it there, his hands lingering in Josh's hair, stroking his nape with strong, work roughened fingers. Josh's thoughts stopped, his head instinctively tilting back, eyes drifting closed as he remembered that this too was allowed, even here in the open where people might see. And at that thought, he brought his own hands up, dragged Giniw's face to his and kissed him mindlessly.

The heat of Giniw's mouth on his, the taste, made him arch up towards the other man. He freed a hand to pull at Giniw's leather shirt, frustrated by its lack of buttons and then distracted by the warm, soft, suppleness of it. He concentrated instead on getting the gown like thing he had been wearing off his shoulders so that he could press his oversensitive, newly healed nipples against the leather and feel it drag over them as Giniw pushed him down.

What happened then was half lazy exploration—on

Giniw's part—and half screaming frustration on Josh's. He wasn't accustomed to the niceties of courtship, he was used to getting it over with quickly before you were caught, and Giniw's attempts to slow the pace had him cursing and trying to get the other man to move faster by force. There were points when he wasn't sure if it was more wrestling than sex, except that that, too—being held down, fighting back, struggling against the unyielding hardness of Giniw's body—was almost too erotic for him to bear. In the end he wasn't sure whether it was the contest itself or his final surrender that did the trick, but when he was finally permitted to come, pinned, wrists bruisingly held above his head, Giniw was not far after.

They lay on fur and the tree whispered above their heads. "You're getting strong," said Giniw at last, his expression half smug, half tentative.

"I walked today," Josh murmured in agreement. "Only down to the river, but...yes. I'm feeling better."

"One day we must do that when you are fully recovered. I will need to keep myself in training." Giniw sat up, leaning against the tree, and pulled a limp and satisfied Josh into his arms. They lay as they had done at first, Josh propped up against his chest and encompassed by his arms. "You *will* marry me then? I am glad."

"Oh!" Josh sat up, woken from his contented stupor as though he had had a bucket of cold water thrown over him. Had he just agreed to get married? Damn! He kept thinking of himself as an Irish sodomite and not as...whatever it was Opichi had called him. Did Giniw think of him as he would of a woman? Did he expect the same kind of chastity he would expect from a woman? The same kind of obedience?

And Opichi—she was expecting someone who would look after the babies and help around the house, keep respectful silence, and not feel hard done by when he lay awake in the dark and listened to his man make love to someone else. He wasn't sure he could do that. Whatever

159

they called him, in his mind he was a man. A man with his own career, with the memory of command, and the love of battle.

"Y'see," he said, "among my people men like me'd be hanged if anyone found out about us. Marriage...we're not allowed it. Though we pretend sometimes, everyone knows it isn't real."

"It is real here. We do not waste people like you white men do. We would go back to my village and hold a dance, and everyone would be glad for us. They would think I was fortunate, for an *agokwa* is a strong wife and an important person."

Josh's heart twisted within him again. He ran his hands up Giniw's muscular arms and imagined a future of openness and respect. A family of his own, the baby and her brothers and sisters treating him as one of their parents. No more death, no more hiding, no more lies.

No more Peter. No more even the hope of him, even the glances snatched at a distance, even the moments of awkward, embarrassed friendship around someone else's dinner table.

But how wise would it be to go back, to try and live off the crumbs from Peter's table, to watch while he married and to remain a ravenous shadow by his side, slaking hunger in the back rooms of sordid pubs until he was finally beaten to death or hanged or died of a chance caught pox, bringing disgrace on his friends?

No, he couldn't go back to that. He would be mad to choose that over the prospect of peace and happiness. But still...*Peter*.

Chapter Twenty-two

"You bloody parasite! Whose cock did you suck to get *this* whitewash pushed through? I know you haven't stopped at that wizened little pen-pusher. It must be an admiral at least this time!"

Peter stopped and gaped, well aware of the crowds around him looking on. He had been adjusting his sword-belt, feeling relieved and yet a little dazed that the verdict of the court martial was that he had done right in surrendering. Captain Joslyn's account of the *Seahorse*'s sorry state when she was left alone to fight off the four remaining French ships made his own actions seem a little more tolerable to him than he had been allowing himself to believe, of late. The restoration of his sword and his rank had brought with them the first pleasant reflections he had been able to allow himself for months.

But it seemed he had been premature in supposing that his luck had changed, for here was Captain Walker with a face purple as a blood-clot, shouting things that could not be mentioned in front of a crowd of Sunday strollers come down to take the sea air.

"Damne! When I heard you'd both gone down—you and that filthy little catamite of yours—I knew it was the work of Providence... 'Vengeance is mine, saith the Lord. I will repay!' Trust our limp-wristed courts to bollocks even that up!"

Peter wasn't sure whether it was the slight to Josh, or just an instinctive dislike for being shouted at, but he had drawn himself up and replied coldly, "You sir, are drunk. You must be, for nothing else could excuse this behavior," before he had time for thought.

"Do not try and come the moralist with me, you dirty sod!"

Borne up on a tide of what certainly felt like righteous fury, Peter punched Walker in the mouth, dimly aware of the gasps of the spectators, but more viscerally aware only that Walker had had this coming for *years*. "How dare you!" Peter exclaimed in a voice of ice. "You will take this insult back immediately, or I will have satisfaction to the full limit of my power."

Walker's pale eyes gleamed, and he hunched forwards like a bear readying itself to strike. "That will suit me very well, Mr. Kenyon. I shall be glad to knock your brains out with my own hand. My second will be Reverend Jenson. Have yours call on him at any hour, but do not be tardy, or I will consider the vice of sodomy joined by that of cowardice."

Peter was still fuming at dawn as he waited on the beach. The morning promised to be beautiful; sun rising in a faint gray haze, the breeze bringing scents of sugar cane and rum to sweeten the sea's faint scent of seaweed and sharpness.

Joslyn stood beside him, in a civilian's yellow waistcoat and a coat of brocade as if to clearly signal that this was a private, not a naval matter, though everyone present was of the navy, including Dr. O'Connor, lately returned with the *Nimrod*. When Peter thought about it, he was touched that both men had been willing to come out on his side, for the accusation against which he defended himself was often enough in itself to lose a man his friends.

The sun slipped above the horizon in an arc of boiling gold. Bermuda's harsh dawn chorus reached new levels of stridency. On the shining sea, just within sight, a merchantman rocking at anchor began to let down her sails, white as ice, and wing towards harbor.

Walker's party arrived, and the two seconds went aside, smoothing an area of sand and marking out its limits with tape and small rocks, and it occurred to Peter, who had seen Walker fight before, that there wasn't a great deal of hope that he would survive this match. He felt the thought should disturb him more, but it seemed inconsequential. After all, he had lost his ship and his friend, and if he died here, he would not have to go to Emily's wedding this afternoon. A great deal of social awkwardness would thus be avoided.

Walker stripped off his coat and waistcoat, folded them neatly and placed them on a small rug that had been brought for the purpose. He received his sword from Joslyn with a glare of disapproval and the words "You too, eh?" But as Walker stepped over the line into the marked out area, his surliness transformed into a grin of anticipation. "Shall we?"

The sand was damp and firm. Peter stepped over the line and watched his opponent with a feeling of peace, everything falling away in the immediacy of the moment. There was a kind of joy in it, and he had time to wonder whether this was the feeling Walker had become addicted to, the moment he sought to attain in every deed of his life, driven as a man by the craving for opium or the bottle.

His mind quite clear, he saw the flutter as O'Connor dropped the handkerchief, read the intent in Walker's muscles as the larger man lunged forward, and pivoted out of the way. But Walker's lunge was a feint and as Peter turned he barely blocked the second stroke in time. Trying for a quick disarmament, he ran his hand-guard up the blade and twisted lock at the top, but Walker's grip was strong. Smiling, he punched Peter in the face with his other

163

hand, stepped back and pulled his sword, metal shrieking against metal, out of the lock. As Peter was still reeling with surprise from the illegal blow, Walker stepped in and thrust the point of his sword straight through Peter's left shoulder.

The pain, and the sheer injustice of it, broke Peter's mood of calm. He could hear the seconds quarreling; Joslyn insisting that honor was satisfied, Jenson claiming that death would be a mercy. Blood dripped from his fingers onto the white sand of the beach as he danced out of Walker's range. The man was a bull, and he knew it—his heaviness was a coating of fat on top of sheer muscle. He lunged again, and this time Peter was ready for the feint, leaped inside it and scored a long line of red along Walker's upper arm. But the injury was cosmetic only, barely a scratch, and as Peter retreated again out of range, he felt the first wave of dizziness that comes with blood loss, and understood that he had neither strength nor skill, nor—now—stamina over the other man.

Well, he could hope for luck. But at that thought he remembered that he was fighting this duel in defense of a lie. He *was* a guilty sod. If God himself guided these contests to determine that the right man won, He was surely guiding Walker now, unless repentance counted for anything. Were not sins wiped out when you turned from them? He had put Josh aside, he had intended to marry, live a blameless life. Why would he be punished for that? He had done the right thing.

Blocking a swinging cut that came in overhead, his muscles burning as he tried to prevent Walker from pushing their joined blades into his face, he realized suddenly that he was tired of doing the right thing. He would be grateful when this was over and he could lie in death's long sleep and never wake again. His grip faltered, his head bowing as he let Walker drive him backwards towards the ring of tape, defeat, and dishonor.

"*Sir!*"

God! That voice! Far away and tiny with distance though it was. Oh, God, it sounded so much like... Distracted, he turned his head and Walker kicked his feet out from beneath him. As he tumbled there was a brief, confused glance of the distant merchantman now mooring in the harbor of St. George; frantic movement on her deck, a figure in scorched, blackened and battered Royal Navy coat, with hair as red as autumn. And as he fell he was already twisting away from the vicious downward slice of Walker's blade, disbelief and anguish and joy making him feel invulnerable, inhumanly strong.

His own sword cut the tendon at the back of Walker's knees. Walker fell like a mountain, Peter only just rolling out of the way in time. Reason would have told him to stop—he did in fact hesitate—and then Walker, kneeling, stabbed him a second time in the same arm and his parry, wild, inaccurate, emotional, glanced off Walker's collarbone and rebounding, severed the great vein in his neck. Walker dropped his sword, wrapped his fingers around his throat, trying to keep the blood in, gasping, his lips turning blue.

Then O'Connor pushed past Peter to try what he could do. Joslyn warily took the sword from Peter's hand and guided him away. "To say this is a happy outcome seems disrespectful," he said carefully, "but if not happy, it is unmistakable that you were aided by a greater hand than your own. No man here can have any doubt that the accusation was false."

"*I* say it's happy," O'Connor interrupted. He was, as quite usual for a man of his profession, covered and sodden with blood, and his loose hair clung about his face as he smiled a most un-doctor-like smile. "The world is better off without him. Now let me see to that arm."

Something, whether love or life returning, had buoyed him up, but when O'Connor stripped the shirt from the deep wounds in his arm, prodded them and took out a long needle and thread, Peter found the nearest stone to sink down on, shaky with amazement and shock.

"Was that our young friend from the *Macedonian*?" said Joslyn, echoing his own incredulity, as the stitches went in in a succession of piercing and tugging pains. "What an astonishing thing! And a delightful one. I wonder what it can mean."

Peter also wondered. Delivered to his house by a fatherly Joslyn and directed to regain some of his lost blood through sleep and food, instead he took a careful bath and waited on tenterhooks for the knock on the door that surely must come. It surely must come. Josh would know, wouldn't he, that the first thing he ought to do on returning home was come to Peter's side. He would know that, wouldn't he?

But Peter's bath came and went, and he shaved, sent the housemaid out to buy a wedding present and a bottle of Josh's favorite claret, dressed in his best dress uniform for the wedding and sat down to a solitary dinner. After which, feeling alternately certain that he had mistaken that glimpse, and that Josh was still dead after all, and miserably abandoned if he was alive, Peter slept for an hour. When he woke it was time for the wedding, and as he left, he found a card had been delivered into the hall:

Finding it hard to convince Commodore and Bank I am not dead. Have been invited to the dance, post wedding. Will speak to you then. I have something to ask you.

Andrews

PS, Condolences re Miss Jones.

Peter stood with his tricorn in one hand and this terse

little note in the other and laughed. He laughed until the tears rolled, and if it was a somewhat hysterical laugh, well, there was no one else in the room to hear it and disapprove.

Chapter Twenty-three

Light sparkled from the chandeliers, shedding rainbows on the peach satin gown, coral-wound blond head and swanlike neck of Mrs. Emily Robinson. She was looking particularly well tonight, Peter thought, as he led with the left foot, brushed past her right shoulder and triumphantly realized he had executed the complex figures of the Duke of Rutland's Delight without faltering or failure. He was not unconscious that the exercise had lent a fine glow to Emily's cheek, a sparkle to her eyes, and a most becoming heave to her swell of white bosom, and the thought that these things now belonged to somebody else gave him a pang of unworthy regret.

The dance over, he tucked her small hand into the crook of his elbow as he escorted her back to her husband. Emily glanced at him, then away again; too well brought up, or too indifferent to speak first, and he cast around for something to say. Unfortunately he had used "M*y* congratulations, I hope you will be very happy" already. As the silence went on, he could feel a sort of ebbing away of her enjoyment, like a tide going out. *I am in your debt for my rescue?* Too embarrassing? *I will of course pay your father back as soon as I may?* Too mercenary?

"Did you say there would be fireworks?" he asked, with a feeling of achievement.

"Oh yes," she removed her hand from his arm and

smiled, "Mr. Summersgill felt that as I was the only child for whom he would have to provide a dowry, I should be sent off in style. He is a good man."

"He is." Peter smiled at her, glad that on this one point they saw eye to eye. It was a small start to what might become a friendship, but it eased some of his anxiety over whether he had treated her shamefully or not. One could not say, "I hope you do not resent me for my unsuccessful pursuit", but this was a welcome indication in that direction.

"Captain." Of the two of them, Adam looked the more glowing, as release from his own anxiety made him seem again the exuberant, amiable man who had embarrassed Peter with his praise so long ago on the *Nimrod*. "I was so glad to hear of the results of the inquiry and to have Captain Andrews unexpectedly return from the dead...well, we feel very blessed. Perhaps unfairly blessed."

"Not at all." Peter shook the outstretched hand with real good will. "The best man won."

Turning to observe the dancing, Peter saw that Josh was joining the set with a scrawny, underfed creature with a coiffure whose glossy blackness seemed to be rubbing off on her collar. Her looks seemed to guarantee that this was the only time in the evening she would be asked to dance, and while he admired the gallantry of it, Peter was a little worried that Andrews was raising expectations he had no intention of fulfilling. It would be hard for her not to be in a fair way already to be in love with the tall young captain with the wicked smile and lively brown eyes. Josh, too, was looking particularly fine tonight.

It was so good to have him back! The world seemed brighter for having him in it, spiky opinions, brilliant smile, and all. That had not changed, though the man himself had, in some way Peter had not been able to pinpoint. He found himself constantly watching, trying to work it out, alternately fascinated and guilty at being so obsessed. Jealous—in case this confidence was a sign that Josh had someone new to love—and ashamed at his jealousy. He wished Andrews every happiness—of course he did. Had even hoped he would find someone who suited him better, but still the suspicion made him itch beneath the skin, made him want to find this new lover and punch him in the teeth because Josh was...

Was not his. Not any more. Shaking his head, annoyed, Peter reminded himself that he was here to enjoy the evening, praise the music and perhaps to look for a wife. *Not* to lose himself in reverie over a relationship which had been over for months and had never been legal nor moral in the first place. Something he should remember with abhorrence, not fondness. Certainly not with yearning.

Admiring the grace with which Josh moved, the way his new dress uniform fit from good strong shoulders to well-shaped calves in smooth, strokeable white silk stockings, he made the mistake of looking up, straight into the man's eyes. There was the snap of a connection. Laughter, then sudden surrender and heat; a giving everything up, an invitation. Peter's mouth went dry and his heart pounded as the diffused sexual delight of the past hour focused itself upon a willing target. Then Josh looked away, smirking, his head high and his step triumphant, and Peter came back to himself, feeling delirious and weak willed and lost.

The floor had cleared for Governor Bruere and Lady Emelia Wooton, Dowager Duchess of Salisbury, to dance the latest minuet, in a stately, exquisite parade of control and grace, when Peter at last managed to hunt the elusive Andrews to ground. Deprived of his endless stream of partners, he was sitting at a small card table, lounging against the back of his chair. He raised his eyebrows at Peter and said, "Join me for a smoke, sir?"

"Glad to."

Outside it was blissfully cool. They lit their cigars at the sconces by the door and then took a turn into one of the garden's long shaded walks, where starlight slipped in bluish dapples through the white stars of jasmine. In the comparative privacy, Peter took off his hat and wig, ruffled his fingers through his hair, sighing as the night breeze blew through it.

Amber light gilded Josh's face for a moment as he breathed in, his eyes closed, luxuriating perhaps in the burn of smoke in his lungs, perhaps in the peace. "So," he exhaled a silver cloud into the moonlight, "she married someone else. How are you holding up?"

For a moment, Peter was overcome with the sensation that everything in the world had come right at once. An instant of perfection, sharp as the strike of the hammer against a bell, and even after it passed, the bustling gardens resonated with its harmonics, wringing fresh sweetness from the cool air, the scent of jasmine and the sea. "It would do no good to tell you I'm having a miserable time, would it?" Peter smiled.

Josh cocked his head to one side and gave Peter a considering look, before his mouth drew up into an infuriatingly smug smile. "Not pining away for love of her?"

There was no conscious decision behind it—it just felt natural to reach out and trace that smile with his fingers—it quirked up a little more beneath his touch. Feeling the realness of Josh's mouth, the warm skin and smile, Peter sighed. Josh was not dead. In a strange, confused way, that must mean that Peter, too, was free to be alive once more.

"I think on the whole I'm relieved," he said.

The look in Josh's onyx eyes was speculative, amused, as though he was weighing up an opponent at sea; guessing from small clues how his mind worked. Then he tilted his chin up a little and gently kissed Peter's fingertips.

"Captain Andrews!" Peter snatched his hand away, and watched Josh's smile die with something of the same feeling he had had when they lowered the *Seahorse*'s colors. But this was not...not the place, not the time, suppose someone saw?

"I was going to say how very relieved I was myself," said Josh, his eyes dark and soft and reproachful, "but am I to guess my interest wouldn't be welcome?"

Before Peter could reply the ballroom began to empty, and for a while all either of them could decently do was to bow and smile at various acquaintances as they slowly meandered past. Taking Josh's elbow, he steered him out of the current of people. "Not here," he said. And then, when they were well out of the crowd. "You know Walker accused me...us. He said in public that you were my catamite."

Josh's look of pathos became almost a parody of surprise.

"I killed him," Peter said, "but you know the power of rumor."

The surprise gradually settled into an expression of deep inward unease, as Josh looked to one side, his eyelids crescents over downcast eyes. "I do. I'm sorry—I'll be more careful in future. But you haven't answered my question."

They turned onto a path that lead uphill to the carefully groomed "wilderness" beyond the formal gardens. At the top there stood a small folly, its pillars white in the starlight and its curved back gleaming with mother of pearl, imitating the huge, moving glimmer of the ocean that lay behind it.

Catching sight of it, Peter felt a great yearning for the cleanness of life at sea—dangerous at times, but *simple*. Not like this tangle in which he found himself. Oh, his own hand might have woven it, but it had long since become too complex for him to unravel.

Sitting down heavily in the crystal-studded "cave" beneath the "temple" provoked a great burst of scent from the chamomile bench; too sweet for the bitterness that seemed to have lodged in his chest. "I don't understand," he admitted. "Why are you starting this between us again? Didn't you tell me yourself that you expected me to leave you, to find a wife? Was that not what you wanted? Why would you say that to me if it was not what you wanted?"

"Because you could escape." Josh's tone was characteristically earnest. "You could leave the underworld completely behind and be free. The last thing I wanted was to drag you down into the mire with me."

"Damn it!" Peter was stung by the thought as if by a mosquito. He had *known* this from the moment, in the hold of the *Seahorse*, when he worked out that Josh's silence was an attempt to shield him from his own actions. When had he forgotten that? When it became convenient to do so? Was he such a cad? "Damn it! I want your honesty, not lies! I'm not a woman. Stop trying to protect me!"

"I'm not a woman either, sir. Which, I venture to suggest, is the problem."

The little dry remark stopped Peter's anger in its tracks, made him chuckle despite himself—despite the frustration and the terrible, nagging sensation that he had been an utter bastard and hadn't even noticed.

"So..." Peter said, carefully. "You didn't *want* me to leave at all. You only *said so* because you wanted to see me safe; none the worse for a youthful folly, now left behind?"

Sitting down beside him, Josh twisted his face into a grimace. The skirts of his coat fell over Peter's knee; the touch startling, making his blood jump, then race. "That's a little too Jesuitical for me, sir," Josh said softly. "I did want you to leave *because* I wanted to see you safe. I wanted you to leave because only a monster would want to be responsible for destroying and damning a good man like you, and I...I didn't want to be a monster."

"My God!" Peter said, shocked at his own insensitivity, at not seeing and responding to the depths of his own lover's pain. He had said he wanted to give affection—insisted upon it, even—and then never even attempted it. "I failed you in every conceivable way, didn't I? I used you like a whore. I made promises you at least knew I never intended to keep, and I fulfilled your every low expectation, confirming you in the belief that you had the right to nothing at all."

What could he say? There simply weren't words enough to make this right. So he bent his head back to watch a flight of brilliant red and green fireworks and groped for Josh's hand, feeling its warm solidity with a jolt of desire and doubt. "All the time I believed I was doing what you wanted—what *everyone* wanted, and the truth was I was merely caving under pressure. Protecting myself at your expense. I wonder that you came back! What have I ever given you but grief?"

Josh smiled a lopsided smile. "When I told you what I was," he said slowly, "I thought you'd do as everyone else had done; you'd despise me. Will I tell you what my expectations really were? Hatred and the noose. It was a revelation that you'd still talk to me, let alone be my friend. Never would I have *dared* hope we'd be lovers. But you— you gave me every last dream but one—and that one I fought tooth and nail not to tell you, in case you destroyed yourself trying to give me that, too."

Peter fought for composure as he wriggled backwards to lean against the dry, knobbly wall of the cave. Josh's shoulder pressed against his as he too made himself comfortable, neither of them looking at one another, both quite well aware that they were now touching in several places.

"Tell me your last dream," he said, "and let me see if I can risk it."

Josh was silent. Only his breathing lifted the chest pressed against Peter's arm. They stayed that way a long time, and then Josh said slowly, "Let me tell you about the *Macedonian*'s destruction and my rescuers first, or you won't understand how I came to change my mind. Why I'll speak now when I wouldn't then."

"Oh yes! The fire-ship. My God! I've never seen anything so splendid or so appalling. You deserve to be made post for that—or to be horsewhipped, I can't decide which. How did you come through it alive?"

"Well, sir, I'm not so sure." Josh rested his head against the wall and said "All I remember was fire and then something went 'boom', and the next thing I know, I'm being dragged out of the water by a red Indian brave and his wife. Giniw and Opichi. Better friends I never had. They looked after me, and when I was recovered they asked me to stay. And d'you know what?"

His gaze slid sideways to rest on Peter's face, and he raised his eyebrows slightly, challengingly. Amused, Peter obediently retorted, "What?"

"Giniw asked me to be his wife."

"No!" Peter made a face of astonishment and snorted indecorously into his hand, his shoulders shaking with laughter. "What a farce! But, I mean—he must have known?"

Josh's mouth pulled into a line of disapproval, almost a flinch. Peter was conscious of having made a dreadful mistake. What he had interpreted as an outrageous tale of foreign perversity must clearly have meant something quite different for Josh. Something important. "I'm sorry," he said at once. "I shouldn't laugh. Of course he must have known."

"Yes. He did." For a moment Josh's whole body expressed the same beaten, cowed misery he had carried as a midshipman when they first met, when he first told Peter what he was. "And I had the devil of a time explaining to them both why it shocked me so. You see..." Josh's mouth thinned further but his shoulders straightened. He raised his head, and Peter found himself on the end of a glare threatening as a cocked pistol. There was a glow in those dark eyes like the muzzle-flash of a cannon, and Peter was

forcibly reminded that he was no longer facing an inferior—
in rank or in anything else.

"You see, sir, he would have been *proud* to have such a
wife. Their people—the Anishinabe people—would have
honored him for it, because they think men like me are *holy*.
Different, yes. But not *abominable*."

His voice shook with disappointment and anger.
Launching himself to his feet, he strode out into the dark.
Peter's heart lurched with loss, and he was half way out of
his seat in pursuit when Josh returned, braced himself
belligerently against the grotto and said, "They think we're
holy. A bridge between man and woman, man and God.
Here's an outrageous thing: They think that God made us
like this because God wants us like this! And I thought...I
thought perhaps they were right.

"Maybe I don't have to bring you eternal torment as a
price for my love. Maybe I'm not a *poison* I have to protect
you from. What if I, too, could be a blessing? What if I
could make you happy? I'm sorry, sir..." His nostrils flared
and he gave Peter a withering look of contempt that made
Peter's breath catch in his throat. "I'm sorry that you find
the idea so very *funny*."

For a moment all Peter could feel was relief—that Josh
had come back, that he was still there, not exactly shouting,
but doing as good an impression of it as was possible
without raising one's voice. Relief gave way to
astonishment, to a warm burst of something bright in his
heart and his belly as he began to understand that this tirade
was a declaration of love. It was only when these two
pleasures had ebbed a little that he had space to realize he
hadn't yet tried to apologize. "Josh..."

But Josh was in no mood to listen. "No!" he said,
cutting off the explanation with a sweep of his hand.
"You're going to hear me out. I waited 'til we were here to
tell you. I wanted dancing, fireworks, darkness, I thought it
would be romantic. Don't *laugh*! And you royally fucked

that up, sir, but I'm going to say it anyway. You want to marry? So do I. And you might be a total bastard at times, but *I love you. S*o marry me."

Oh! Peter thought. *Oh God!* And there was a pause, like the pause—infinitesimal and yet so very long—between the order to fire and the first broadside of a full fleet action. "I'm sorry?"

"With all due respect, sir," said Josh, close examination revealing, behind the threat of his expression, a thrumming of nervous hope, "you heard me the first time. Peter Kenyon, *will you marry me*?"

Chapter Twenty-four

A pause.

Peter thought, aghast, that it was no wonder Josh had defeated a French ship of the line. His head for unorthodox tactics was frightening. "If we went to church and asked the priest to marry us, we would end up being hanged in one noose," he said, feeling both affronted at being put in the woman's place in this, and yet dimly, shamefully relieved. "So you cannot be suggesting that. I am not assuming again that I know what you mean. Elaborate."

"Yes, sir." Josh snapped to attention, faintly ridiculous given the circumstances. "As I see it, there are three options. One, I persuade a captain I know, of my persuasion, to marry us under our own names at sea. Two, we travel to Giniw's country and marry by their rite." He flashed an aggressive smile—daring Peter to laugh. "I'd consider that pretty unfeeling towards my rescuers, frankly."

"And three," the smile softened and warmed, "and this is my favored option, you give me your word before God to forsake all others, to cleave to me until we die, and I swear the same by you, and that's enough for me."

Peter rubbed the bridge of his nose. This was not something to be treated lightly. He no longer had the excuse of simply not having thought about the issues. It would not be a youth's rash impulse—throwing his life away upon a whim. It would be a man's decision, fully thought out and acceded to by body, mind, and soul. A frightening thought. "What would you do if I said no?"

"With respect, sir, you do not need to take that into consideration. The issue is what *you* want. If you do not think the game is worth the candle, it is enough to say so. The consequences to me are not your concern."

"Humor me."

Josh turned away, bowing his head slightly; slumped shoulder and rounded cheek in shadow. "I would grieve. Of course. But then I'd go back and marry someone who did want me."

Peter laughed, concealing how uneasy that remark had made him feel. It hadn't occurred to him before tonight that Josh might have other options than merely to wait for his pleasure. He supposed he had been relying on Josh to be there—a certainty held in reserve. The thought of having to turn his back on that, of ruling a line under this affair and meaning it this time, was as frightening as the thought of rejecting the laws of God and man to embrace it.

He remembered that it had been Josh's voice which startled him out of despair during the duel, gave him strength to fight for his honor and win. Where would he find that strength if Josh deserted him? "But we could still be friends?"

"I don't know," Josh said unexpectedly and came back to sit by Peter's side once more, putting his head in his hands. "What would it mean to be friends, if I was there and you were here? Opichi and Giniw...they're good people. I wouldn't mess them about. So I think...I think it's this or goodbye. I can't carry on being what I was, not now I know there's something better."

This, too, was an intolerable thought. Peter had grown used to Josh simply being there; as little to be remarked upon, as indispensable and, he had supposed, as inseparable as his own soul. Turning to reassure himself that Josh was

179

in fact still there, he found the younger man with his fingers underneath his wig, clutching at his hair.

"So, that's a 'No, let's just be friends' then, sir. Is it?"

It should be. Peter knew it should be. How would he ever be able to look himself in the eye again, knowing now how the world would condemn his sordid secret, if they knew it? Better not to have a sordid secret. Perhaps among savages such things might happen, but that didn't make them possible for gentlemen. He must say no.

Opening his mouth, a white star of panic burst beneath his breastbone at the thought and rose to choke off the word unsaid. He could not—physically—force it out.

Peter did not like being dictated to by his feelings. Making a tactical retreat, so that he could consider, approach the problem from a different angle, he shook his head to dislodge the obstruction in his throat and said, "I'm...taken aback, Josh, I need to..."

Josh took his hands out of his hair, without tearing too much of it out, and looked at him with a puppyish expression that made him feel accused and—in consequence—angry. "You need to get her back before the wind, before you set a course? Fair enough. I know it's an awful lot to ask, and I *want* you to think about it. I want you to be sure."

He stood up, paused, looked down at Peter's upturned face with a smile almost comically hopeful, sweeter than any expression Peter had yet seen on his face. "I'll leave you to contemplate, then. Goodnight, sir."

He launched himself out into the dark, his footsteps drawing away. Calmly drawing away, after having shaken Peter's world to splinters. Damn him!

Damn him! Peter thought viciously, launching himself out onto paths lined with colored lanterns he didn't see, through boiling groves of hot, tropical flowers he did not smell. Damn Andrews! This was all his fault. All his fault that Peter's dream—of a son to follow him in the service, of a daughter whom he would cherish and live to see with a loving family—seemed now as beyond his grasp as the moon. A clean conscience. Was that too much to ask? Other people seemed to achieve it... Other people who had not been exposed, early in their lives, to the temptation, to the *contagion* of a man of Josh's sort.

Maybe that was why the sodomites had to be executed—because if you let them live you ended up...you ended up loving them. And then...and then your life was ruined, and you became a living mockery of everything you stood for, everything you believed in. Maybe, instead of extending the hand of friendship, he *should* have turned Josh in. He should have...

Seen him hanged.

He reached the wall of the gardens, threw open the door and burst through. Breathing hard, aware that—pursued by love—he had fled in panic, he tried to touch that thought again. He should have turned Josh in; seen him hanged? Just when he thought his own mind could not appall him more he thought, *And you still should. If it was your duty then, it is no less your duty now.*

The thought had a black plausibility. He knew that he was being given a final opportunity to repent. No—no, not that. For he had already repented, had he not? He had repented, and his life had been returned to him, during the duel. Now he was being given the chance to *prove* his new righteousness. If it was wrong to say "yes" to Josh, then it was also wrong to continue to allow him to live.

"No!" he said aloud to the night, as he throttled on his own conscience, on the merciless certainty of what he had to do to become the man he thought he had always been. "Oh, God! Oh, God! Josh!"

He stood transfixed, spitted by horror and heartbreak. But you *had to* do what was right, or what kind of man were you? Nothing was more important than that. Nothing. The greater the sacrifice, the more he could be sure of the purity of his motives—and this, this would be the ultimate in obedience. It was, surely, required of him. His restored life was proof of that. Restored to do good, to be a good Christian, to be zealous against the enemies of the faith and to...

But I can't.

It was like drowning—the more he thrashed, the more it closed over his head, the harder he found it to breathe or to think. Before he was aware he was moving, he had set off back up the street towards the mansion. He needed advice; impartial, compassionate, worldly-wise advice. Advice he could trust, and Summersgill...

How could he possibly go to Summersgill with this?

He stopped. The wall of the gardens was high and gray at his shoulder, on the other side stood featureless houses with fan windows making down-turned mouths against the darkness. Further down the street the looming stone shape that was All Souls Church broke the skyline with an Anglo-Saxon square tower and a weather vane in the shape of a two-masted ketch.

Need drove him to it. Pushing the door open brought him into a thicker, more private darkness; a smell of frankincense and dust. The whitewashed walls were bare of ornament and the roof invisible in the gloom. His heels rapped sharply on the tiles, making him feel as if he was intruding. There was an inhabited aura about the soaring vault of a room, as though he was trespassing in someone's bed chamber and, if he was too loud, he would wake them.

Choosing a pew at random, he sat down. "I can't," he said.

As if the darkness had been a sleeping dragon, he felt it wake and curl around him. Its gaze was heavy. "I can't," he said again—trying to make it understand; trying to make *God* understand that he was too weak, to plead that this cup be taken away from him...

Except that it hadn't turned out so well the last time

someone prayed that.

All his life he had tried to do what was expected of him. He had been happy with that, certain of what was right and wrong. Love was unimportant—the law was the law. The sodomites must hang, and he must start with Josh, for personal grief and personal anguish must not be allowed to prevent one from doing what was right.

At the thought, he imagined it; he imagined the look on Josh's face when the troops came for him, Peter's statement in their hands, and the pain made Peter double over, shaking his head, his teeth gritted against the hot, shameful tears that threatened to spill. "I can't!"

He could, though. Nothing, physically, prevented him from doing it. Weighty, substantial men in the community would shake his hand and thank him for rooting out corruption in society's midst, for protecting their children. Josh would be hanged and go to hell—as though there could be anything worse for him than receiving such an answer. And Peter would be feted as a champion of morality, who did not scruple to spare even his friends in the cause of justice.

Was that really what God wanted of him? It was...abominable.

If the darkness was a dragon, it now had a claw on Peter's back, pressing him down. "I can't," he whispered, "I can't."

He was struggling for air, fighting against something he was suddenly not sure he understood, for something that seemed incredibly precious and strong—but under this relentless onslaught he could feel it fracturing, and he was terrified of what would happen next. The very fabric of his life was buckling beneath the weight.

Then it broke. "I can't," he said again, forced beyond the point where he could prevaricate, forced into pure honesty, into decision. "I *won't.*"

It was as though his head had broken the surface, and he

could breathe again, after an eternity of suffocation. "If that's what everyone wants of me, I won't do it. It's wrong."

Nothing had changed. He was still a small, hunched figure in the gloom, in a church stripped of anything remotely valuable by the local thieves. But everything had changed.

"I have to do what *I* think is right, not just what society expects of me," he told the darkness, realizing that this was what his heart had tried to tell him all along; that he might have given it lip service before, but now he *understood*. "And I cannot believe what I feel for Josh is wrong." He gravitated towards the huge book chained to the lectern as the world inclined towards its sun, searching for the words that would help him crystallize this understanding into something that could be thought.

The pages were heavy. He skimmed the black print until he found something he could match to his revelation, and when he had found it, it was so basic, so simple that he could not believe he had not thought of it himself: "God is love. Whoever lives in love lives in God, and God in him."

He stroked the edges of the book, then closed it reverently, looked up at the still flame of the hanging lamp, still feeling enveloped in literal revelation, and said, "Thank you."

Not like Jesus' test after all, but like Abraham's—who thought God wanted him to sacrifice his son and found out at the last moment that God was not like that; that God would provide his own sacrifice, and Abraham could take his son home and watch him grow up, just as he so desperately desired.

But, Peter thought, sitting down on the steps of the pulpit with a smile on his face, Abraham had at least offered. He, on the other hand, had said no. He had found a duty he could not do—he was weak and no saint.

He was no saint; he was no more righteous than the next

man—he had only thought so for a very long time, making him a hypocrite as well as a sinner. It felt undeniably freeing to admit it, like taking off all the gold braid at the end of a long evening and stretching the kinks out of his back. Closing his eyes, he leaned against the curving surround of the lectern, carven eagle-feathers digging into his spine.

He had been a hypocrite even in contemplating his "repentance", he realized. Standing in judgment on Josh? Who was he trying to fool? *He* had started the affair between them; *he* had insisted on it becoming physical. He was the one who could not go to an evening's dancing without admiring Josh from a distance, without seeking him out and finding excuses to touch him. All this time he had thought himself merely yielding to Josh's desire, generously giving Josh what he wanted because of course *he* could have no sodomitical tendencies of his own. He was too good a man for that—too normal, too perfect.

Appalling, appalling hypocrisy.

Getting up, he pushed open the door. The night had deepened while he sat thinking, the scent of fireworks and the blazing stars making him think of Bonfire Nights in Britain—parkin held in gloved hands, steaming spiced punch, and near painful bonfire heat on his upturned face. And the inevitable anti-Catholic riot that would follow. It had always been such fun—as long as you were not a Catholic. This was similar. In saying "yes" to Josh, Peter would remove himself from the mob. He would voluntarily place himself among the victims. The thought held more than a little terror.

If he said "no", he knew he could disappear back into the crowd. The rumors Walker had started would be forgotten, in time. If he said "yes", however, if he said "yes" to loyalty and love, yes to honesty, yes to fidelity, they would not hesitate to destroy him and congratulate themselves on doing it.

185

The street led down towards the harbor; a dark tumble of houses and cobbles, and then the sea, stretching out like a great sheet of mercury beneath an elegant curve of moon. He walked down to it, while his revelation seeped into more of his thoughts, making them grow and fit together—like seawater seeping into a dried out hulk, making her timbers swell and the holes close themselves up.

The fact was that whether society would forgive him or not, he didn't have to decide to break his country's law, to earn himself execution—he had *already* done that. If a future with Josh was a future that ended in the noose, it was no more than he had already deserved.

Going down onto the dirty sand of the beach, he walked along the forlorn shape of HMS *Dart*, her masts unstepped, lying on her side. Her bottom was being scraped and covered with tallow against the attacks of shipworm, but it was still sad to see her, looking so hollow and abandoned. He patted her on the keel and thought about the folly of expecting things—people—to work in ways for which they had not been made. As well expect to sail a ship on dry land as expect Josh to fall in love with a woman. As well make laws to tell a cannon ball to float.

At the thought, he glanced over to the pier where their too brief affair had come to its bitter end, and there moonlight struck glimmers on gold braid, the cockade of a hat tipped up to look at him. He could see, in the darkness, only the gold and white sketch of a man, but it was a man he would know at once from the merest glimpse.

Peter swallowed, feeling suddenly exposed—as though they were the only two standing on the round earth, the only ones in all that sky of stars. He began to walk towards the tall white figure, each footstep another jolt to a stomach that was jumping with nerves.

Beneath the wooden walk, leaning against one of the pillars, still barely more than shadows and faint lights, stood Captain Andrews, as neat as a new pin, perfectly turned out as for a surprise inspection, but with half circles of shadow beneath his eyes and a faint smell of rum on his breath.

"Drink, sir?" He offered a stoneware bottle of the stuff. It seemed clear that Josh was expecting a negative answer. Peter was struck by the quiet anguish of Josh's over-controlled gestures and the sullen pride of his appearance; his armor of braid, his hundreds of carefully done up buttons. But Peter had not come to talk to Captain Andrews, and he did not appreciate the defensive distance.

"Take the damn wig off, Josh," he said. "I'm not here to be 'sir'ed—you know that."

Josh gave him a hangdog look, but he took off his hat and set it carefully on the nearest boulder, wig inside it. Then he passed both hands through his hair, leaving it standing up in distressed, hedgehog spines.

It hurt to watch. "If you were so sure I'd say 'no', why did you ask?" Peter asked, torn between anger, pain, and guilt.

"I wanted to know where I stood," Josh said quietly. "I was offered a future, better than I'd imagined possible, but God forgive me, I didn't want it with him; I wanted it with you."

Above, clouds drew away from the moon. Peter drank a mouthful of rum and watched as Josh's hair slowly relaxed into tousled curls; bronze in shadow, and in the light that extraordinary, beautiful shade of cinnamon that made Peter want to bury his face in it and feel its softness on his lips.

No one could say that hair was second best. Nor the downcast eyes now watching the ground—so startlingly dark against such fair skin. The curve of Josh's cheek was dear to him. It made Josh seem so young and vulnerable, when in truth, he could be such a bastard. But Peter could no more do without the bastard at his side, than he could bring himself to finally give up the whole-hearted, wanton, grateful lover.

"Suppose I had come to say yes?"

187

Josh looked up, fiercely. "And have you?"

Since he physically could not say "no", and no more wanted to go on with this charade of half-hearted nothingness than Josh did, it must follow that he had indeed come to say yes. "I have," he said—and oh, God, the relief! The sense of a burden dropped, a long, fruitless, wearisome battle finished at last. Victory or defeat—it didn't matter. It was just over, and he was at peace. "Yes, I have."

Beneath the relief, joy stirred. He met the startled, hopeful gaze with a smile that began as a mere twitch of the lips but spread until his cheeks ached and his eyes watered with delight. This was going to be quite a challenge, and challenge had always excited him. Who needed a tame course—a course so charted, so well trodden, when one could strike out into the unknown, risking the danger? No boy ever ran away to join the navy because he wanted to be safe.

"With respect, sir," Josh leaned forward, his capable, strong hands splayed on the pillar behind Peter, trapping him in the circle of his arms, "I'm not sure I believe you."

Behind Josh, Peter could see the sea moving lazily and the moonlight sliding over its swelling curves. The moist air was hot and the pier's timbers gave out a faint scent of pitch and sunlight. The moment was too sweet for argument, so Peter took hold of Josh's cravat and dragged him forward by it. Josh's lips parted in surprise, and Peter covered the gasp with his mouth, and for a moment it was all metaphors; it was coming home, it was the first drink of water after days of pitiless heat and thirst, and it was also taste, heat, the mad, animal frenzy with which they both scrabbled to get closer; an elbow in a wet spider's web, Josh's shoe landing on Peter's toe; the desperate whining noises he made at the pressure of Peter's tongue; pleading, demanding. And Peter's answering certainty that he too was *allowed* to want this, to need this, as much as he did.

Allowed in a moral sense at least. Not allowed in any

sense that made it wise to make love in a public place where every courting couple and their mothers might see. "Josh... Oh... Wait... Stop!"

Josh separated himself briefly from the tight knot of limbs, the possessive triumph in his eyes making a shock of glorious, erotic surrender sing and seethe in Peter's blood. "Prove it to me?"

What the hell was he letting himself in for? He wanted to find out at once. "I will," Peter said eagerly, "but not here. At home. In my own bed."

Josh lifted a hand, gently brushed back the errant lock of hair that was always getting in Peter's eyes, his chest heaving with desire, but his touch tentative, tender. "I can't believe it." There was such naked adoration in his gaze that Peter felt almost embarrassed, as if he should say something self-deprecatory to restore the balance, to stop the gods from getting jealous. "I've dreamed these things before. I've dared believe it before...and then I wake up."

It was good there was no reproach in Josh's tone, because Peter felt the stab of shame all too deep without it. How many singular moments of Josh's misery was he responsible for? No. No he would not think about that now; he was too much of a sailor to waste time on the past. The present had to be seized. "He who hesitates is lost, Mr. Andrews. You *will* believe it, I assure you."

Josh stooped to retrieve his lost shoe. When he turned back, he seemed to have regained his composure with it. He insinuated himself just close enough for Peter to feel invaded, tilted his head to one side and watched Peter's face with a frankly admiring look, the worship clothed in playfulness. "I'm not an easy man to impress, Mr. Kenyon. What makes you think that a night of unbridled sexual perversion is going to change my mind?"

"Hm." It was hard to fight the desire—to laugh from sheer joy, to take the taunting young captain by his lapels, slam him into the pillar and firmly prove to him that he was

189

underestimating the persuasive power of Peter's prowess—but this really was not the place. "Am I to understand you're suggesting more than a single night?"

"I was thinking along the lines of the rest of my life."

The laughter broke free. And yes, free was how Peter felt. Free from social obligations, free from his own ridiculous expectations, from a wearisome hunt for something he didn't really want. Free like a man of war leaving harbor with a stiff wind in her sails and every man aboard looking forward to the adventure. This was no tying down to the earth, no prison of domesticity. It was the life he loved given back to him, perfected by not having to be lived alone. And he had no idea how to express any of that in a way that would not be horribly embarrassing to hear.

"That will be acceptable," he said, and watched with an intense pride as Josh's white smile lit up his face, bright as a hunter's moon. It didn't after all need to be said. Andrews—as always—already understood. No romantic words were required, only the truth, and that, too, was an unutterable comfort. "On my oath before God, Josh, I swear it. If it is within my power—for I am not the master of the sea nor of the Service, but if it is within my human power to arrange, this time I will stay with you for the rest of our lives."

Epilogue

The shutters were closed and the doors locked, Peter's servants sent home. There was no one to see the proud uniforms laying discarded on the floor, no one but Josh to admire Peter's long, elegant form spread out on the bed like an offering, lamplight gold on the sheen of sweat over his heaving chest, drowning in the darkness of his pleasure-drugged, dilated eyes.

But Josh, kneeling over him, sinking slowly, inch by inch, onto his hard cock, felt as though the whole world was watching. He leaned down, feeling his own prick slide luxuriously against Peter's sweat and oil damp belly and captured Peter's little, breathless whimpers in his own mouth. Peter's hands let go their death-grip on the sheets and closed bruisingly on Josh's thighs, mutely begging for more.

"Mine," Josh gasped, looking down fiercely at Peter's need.

"Yours," Peter replied, awestruck. "Oh, God, yes. Yours, *please*."

The End

About the Author:

Born in Northern Ireland during the Troubles, Alex Beecroft moved early to Cheshire, where she grew up in the wild countryside of the Peak District. Lots of lonely rambles among heaths and forest made it natural for her to start making up stories. At the age of eleven she started writing them down and she hasn't stopped since.

Alex met her husband in London while working for the Lord Chancellor's Department. Nowadays she lives near the ancient University of Cambridge, where she and her husband are raising two daughters. Alex will tell you that she's thrilled to be doing what she always wanted to do, living her dream of being a writer and published romance author.

You can write to Alex at:
alex.beecroft@lindenbayromance.com

This is a publication of
Linden Bay Romance
WWW.LINDENBAYROMANCE.COM

Recommended Read:

Captial Games by G. A. Hauser

Let the games begin…

Former Los Angeles Police officer Steve Miller has gone from walking a beat in the City of Angels to joining the rat race as an advertising executive. He knows how cut-throat the industry can be, so when his boss tells him that he's in direct competition with a newcomer from across the pond for a coveted account he's not surprised…then he meets Mark Richfield.

Born with a silver spoon in his mouth and fashion-model good looks, Mark is used to getting what he wants. About to be married, Mark has just nailed the job of his dreams. If the determined Brit could just steal the firm's biggest account right out from under Steve Miller, his life would be perfect.

When their boss sends them together to the Arizona desert for a team-building retreat the tension between the two dynamic men escalates until in the heat of the moment their uncontrollable passion leads them to a sexual experience that neither can forget.

Will Mark deny his feelings and follow through with marriage to a women he no longer wants, or will he realize in time that in the game of love, sometimes you have to let go and lose yourself in order to *really* win.

801756

Printed in Great Britain by
Amazon.co.uk, Ltd.,
Marston Gate.